FLORIDALAND GHOSTS

Dylan Clearfield

Floridaland Ghosts ©2000 by Prism Stempien Thomas

Printed in the United States of America

04   03   02   01   00   5   4   3   2   1

ISBN 1-882376-70-6

Cover design by Adventures with Nature

Holt, Michigan

Other titles in the Thunder Bay Press *Tales of the Supernatural* series:
  Haunted Indiana
  Haunted Indiana 2
  School Spirits
  Hoosier Hauntings
  Chicagoland Ghosts
  Haunts of the Upper Great Lakes
  Michigan Haunts and Hauntings

CONTENTS

Dedication:
For my daughters,
Brittany and Heather,
who give spirit to my creations.

NORTHERN FLORIDA

Northwest Coast -- Pensacola Area

The Fordham House at 417 E. Zaragoza. (*Author's photo*)

The Charbonier House where an adventurous young man spent a
terrifying night. *(Author's photo)*

SOME OLD-FASHIONED HAUNTED HOUSES

THE FORDHAM HOUSE

Pensacola is in the extreme southwest of the Florida panhandle only a few miles from the Alabama border. It can be reached on Highway 10 from either the east or the west. There is a quaint section of Old Pensacola called Seville Square in which are located a number of old restored Southern homes, most of which have come under the kindly care of the local historical society. Many of the homes in the Seville Square area are haunted, ranking this as one of the most haunted locations per square foot in the entire country. Fortunately, most of the ghosts here are friendly.

The Fordham House is located at 417 East Zaragoza Street. It was built in 1875 by Don Francisco Moreno as a wedding gift for his daughter, who was about to marry Dr. William Fordham. Throughout the years, ownership of this house has passed through various members of the Fordham family. Ernestine Fordham Nathan was among the last of the Fordhams to live there.She died there as well—in the back room of the house—and is most likely the current resident ghost.

One of the more recent owners of the renovated Fordham House has reported hearing the sound of rustling petticoats and having glimpsed shadowy figures in the mirrors. On one occasion, the owner attempted to restain the floorboards in the back room where Ernestine had died, but discovered that the wood would not accept the new coat.

A particularly chilling occurrence was the time when various pieces of jewelry were left in the front of the house and later turned up in Ernestine's old back room—with all the clasps having been refastened! Apparently, Ernestine still enjoys wearing jewelry on the other side.

The Charbonier Home is located in Seville Square on the southwest corner of Intendencia and Florida Blanca. This story harkens back to the classic ghost tale involving a young man who takes the dare of his friends to stay the night in the sinister building. The man, who we will call Tom, offered to stay a night in the building to prove that it was not haunted.

Soon after being locked inside, Tom settled down for the night in total darkness except for his trusty penlight. He had just dropped off to sleep when a loud noise from the next room jolted him into awareness. Arising to investigate, Tom found that the door to his room was now unlocked and that its pane of window glass had fallen out and shattered on the floor.

The young man returned to his couch and, upon lying back down, was startled to see a strange visitor in the room. It was a frosty globe of red light about the size of a silver dollar, which bounced about the center of the room for the rest of the long night! Could this have been the entity that had frightened a little girl a couple of nights before at a party the owners of the house had given there? She had contacted an unfriendly spirit by ouija board and was given a rather stern warning from it.

After his night in the house, Tom was met by a reporter upon his exit. Tom told his story about the eerie red light. Who or what was this glowing red orb? Could it belong to the spirit of one of the house's earliest occupants, Joseph Charbonier, who twice had been confined to a lunatic asylum? Or could it belong to either Dolores or Pauline who had been the last of the Charboniers to have lived in the manor as housebound recluses? No one knows for sure. Maybe another attempt at the ouija board might give an answer.

Another odd ghost light infests another house on Seville Square, but this light is dazzling blue in color. The Axelson House, in which the scintillating light has been seen, is also on Florida Blanca Street. The building was constructed of cypress logs that Gustave Axelson had cut and shipped by special order in the late nineteenth century. Sometime later the house was occupied by two elderly cousins, both named Margaret.The Margaret cousins were talented women, having succeeded in having a number of their musical compositions pub-

The Axelson House where a mysterious blue light was a common sight for many years. (*Author's photo*)

lished. But they preferred the shelter of their home to gaining notoriety and were content to enjoy their quiet pastimes of sewing and painting watercolors.

In 1940, one of the Margarets died, leaving the home to her spinster cousin whose closest brush with romance had come as a young girl with a 'crush' on a delivery boy. It was with the first Margaret's death in 1940 that the mysterious blue light made its first appearance. The neighbors and passersby noticed it blinking on and off from a first floor window overlooking the Bay.

Since these were war years, blackout restrictions were rigidly enforced and due notice was taken of this curious and brilliant blue light. Government officials set up a lookout point on nearby Zaragoza Street and kept the Axelson House under strict surveillance. After a couple of weeks, the government spies realized that what they were watching was not a secret code nor, for that matter, anything of an earthly nature. They ended up leaving in amused bewilderment.

The blue light continued flickering until the fall of 1963 when just as suddenly as it had begun it stopped. Who or what was this blue light? Could it have been the spirit of the deceased Margaret, which had lingered behind to comfort her dear cousin with whom she had been so close in life?

The Gray House at 314 South Alcaniz Street in Seville Square is also haunted. Soon after Peter and Edna had purchased the home they began to experience strange manifestations. Lights turned on and off by themselves, doors opened and closed, and water poured from turned off faucets.

Peter was not convinced that these events were the workings of a ghost, however, until he laid a pack of cigarettes on a night stand before going to sleep and awoke the next day to find holes pricked into them. The ghost apparently preferred fresh air because it repeatedly re-opened windows around the house after they had been closed. It seems that he is a music lover, too, because on one occasion while Peter and Edna were listening to a concert, a nearby wooden chair rocked in time to the music.

Edna decided to try to contact the spirit by ouija board. The spirit spelled out his name as T-H-O-M-A-S M-O-R-I-S-T-O and revealed that he had been eighty-five years old when he had died and he had lived from 1718 to 1803. Additional confirmation of this was supplied by a medium who also came up with the name Thomas Moristo for the spirit and an age of eighty-five at passing. When examining the history of the house, however, Peter and Edna failed to discover Moristo's named among the previous owners. Nor did the house have the features of a structure that extended as far back as 1802.

Startling evidence was uncovered several years later, however, when research was being done on an adjoining lot. A document from

The haunted Gray House of Thomas Moristo. (*Author's photo*)

1781 was discovered which bore the name of Thomas Moristo. He had been a corporal in the Spanish army and was stationed at nearby Opelousa. Apparently, he had had some attachment to this house in Seville Square after all and decided to remain there, slamming doors, throwing windows open and, upon occasion, speaking to the residents. He obviously still feels at home in the house by the Bay.

STROLLING SPIRITS

Our hunt for ghosts next takes us to Romano Street where both the fashionable and unfashionable can be seen promenading on the sidewalks at night. Among them is a ghost. The ghost's name is—or was—Sarah Wharton, the daughter of Don Irving Wharton, a prominent man in Pensacola in the early 1800s. Even back then the refined and unrefined citizenry of Pensacola took their evening strolls on bustling Romano Street. But then, as now, a person had to be every vigilant of his safety. In the early 1800s, however, the danger was from pirates!

The coasts of Florida were vulnerable to pirate raids and one of the more tempting cities for the buccaneers to assault was Pensacola. It was while Sarah and her father were strolling down Romano Street that one of the pirate raids took place. The young woman's father was an immediate victim of the attack. The pirate leader then grabbed Sarah in order to take her as a prize. Fighting him off, Sarah slashed at the brigand with the hand upon which she wore a large and brilliant diamond. The sharp stone tore one of the pirate's eyes out and, while Sarah still flailed, the diamond did damage to the man's other eye as well. Enraged, the pirate whipped out his cutlass and whacked off Sarah's head. Her lifeless body fell not far from where her father lay. Today, Sarah's ghost can be spotted strolling sadly down Romano Street and sometimes it is only the bright glint of her spectral ring that is seen floating in the air.

A similar fate befell a young maiden on nearby Santa Rosa Island. In this case, however, the young woman involved courted the affections of a dashing buccaneer. The pirate captain with whom she had fallen in love was in the habit of frequenting a harbor cove known as 'Deadman's Hollow.' It was here that the woman made her secret visits to the pirate.

The maiden's father was a wealthy and powerful businessman and he highly disapproved of his daughter's association with such a disreputable character, especially since he had already chosen a wealthy suitor for her from a good family. To prevent any further rendezvous at Deadman's Hollow, the father had his daughter imprisoned in her own bedroom. The young maiden howled and raged, but could not escape her cell until she convinced a sympathetic servant to help her out of her plight. Freed at last, the maiden fled her home and rushed to Deadman's Hollow.

She did not know, however, that the suitor that her father had selected for her had been watching her house and that he had followed her. He caught up with her near Deadman's Hollow and drew her into his arms. Seeing this from afar, the pirate stormed toward the two, thinking that the maiden had found a new lover and was flaunting him before his eyes. Before the woman could even speak, the pirate drew his sword and lopped off her head. He carried her lifeless body back with him to Deadman's Hollow. Can there be any wonder why the spirit of the wrongly-murdered maiden haunts this part of the beach?

The next story comes from the period of the War of 1812. Spain had just relinquished rule over Florida but had been slow in actually handing over the real estate and vacating the property. In order to hasten the Spain's departure, General Andrew Jackson was dispatched to the Pensacola area to evict the Spanish governor from the mansion—in a diplomatic fashion, of course.

Among General Jackson's entourage was a Colonel Morgan who promptly began an affair with the Spanish governor's pretty young daughter. Colonel Morgan and the dark-haired señorita spent a good deal of time together riding along the Gull Point bridle path, which infuriated the outgoing governor. Finally, he confronted the two lovers and, in a fit of rage, shot and killed the young Colonel.

Colonel Morgan was buried with military honors on the Gull Point cliff. The bereaved señorita visited his grave almost every day and spoke softly to her departed lover where he lay in the ground. It was not too long before she herself died, but her spiteful father would not permit her to be buried near her beloved. But not even he could prevent his daughter's ghost from returning to Colonel Morgan's grave. Witnesses have caught brief glimpses of the two lovers in the moonlight as they stroll together along the cliff, joined in the afterlife.

Pensacola Lighthouse which is occupied by a pipe-smoking ghost.
(*Author's photo*)

THE HAUNTED NAVAL YARD

Most people are familiar with the famous Pensacola Naval Base, but not many know about the ghosts who haunt a couple of the buildings on and near the grounds of this base. Pensacola Naval Base has been in existence since 1826, when it was called the Pensacola Navy Yard. Nearby is a lighthouse that has long been reputed to be haunted. No one knows for sure who the ghosts are who occupy this eerie sullen building, but one of them smokes a pipe. The scent of burning pipe tobacco is one of the many manifestations at the site. The lighthouse has since been converted into the living quarters for upper-level officers on the naval base. One of the vice admirals who has lived in the building reported smelling the odor of pipe smoke on many occasions. Others have seen the shade of the pipe-smoking commandant along with a lady friend in white. Marching footsteps, slamming doors, and apparitions have also been witnessed here.

There is another haunted building on the site of the old Pensacola Naval Yard. It is currently the headquarters building for the Naval Education and Training Command. The forty-four-year-old building is a converted naval hospital, which may account for a couple of the odd manifestations. Mysterious and sinister writing has appeared on certain basement walls like: "Help! Let me out" and "Death awaits." What makes these inscriptions particularly ghoulish is that they were written on the doors to the cooler that had been used to store dead bodies.

Mysterious occurrences have also been experienced on the upper floors of the building. Among them is a sickening odor. People here have been accosted by this foul stench while passing by what had formerly been an operating room. It is an odor that comes and goes as if it may be originating from a ghostly gurney being rolled into the operating room.

Another manifestation took place in the copying room where the copy machine went into a fit of turning itself on and off, thwarting the efforts of office people to get their work done. One of the secretaries had a particularly frightening encounter with the ghost. One day when she was in conversation with another person, the picture of her son lifted off her desk of its own accord and flew into the wall several feet away.

The haunted officer's quarters at the Pensacola Naval Air Station
(*Author's photo*)

Another spirit is that of Marine Captain Guy Hall who is seen frequenting Building 16, which in 1926 was an officer's club. Captain Hall was a flight instructor at the Naval Air Station who enjoyed his games of poker. While playing at the officer's club, he was in the habit of picking up his stack of chips in a particularly characteristic way and letting them clatter back down onto the table top.

In 1926, Captain Hall was killed in an untimely air crash at what was then known as Corry Field. But this has not kept him from his beloved poker games at the officer's club. The characteristic sound of his falling stack of chips is still heard on many an occasion. Witnesses have reported hearing this sound when there were neither card games being played nor a visible chip to be found. Hopefully, Captain Hall was dealt a winning hand.

The Naval School of Photography is another building on the base that is frequented by a ghost. This building was formerly an army barracks where a young enlisted man took his life earlier in the twentieth century. His spirit has remained here, however, and its grim moaning can be heard on many nights, tormented by the bleak development that had ended its life prematurely.

It seems that many spirits are still very active in the old Pensacola Naval Yard and the attending lighthouse. Apparently, some of these old soldiers have not completely faded away.

TALLAHASSEE AREA

THE ROSY GHOST

This story is one of those quaint antebellum stories that come from a much quieter time in the period of the deep South's history. It is a romantic story set in the mid-1800s when paddle wheel steamboats still plied the waterways and the grand plantation mansions stood like castles over vast domains of cotton.

This very old story comes from the El Rio Plantation in Suwannee County overlooking the banks of the famous Suwannee River—the river about which Stephen Foster wrote his popular song. The characters in the song reflect well those characters in this story about the 'rosy ghost.'

El Rio Mansion was typical of the great southern mansions of the day. Its huge main section was two stories high and was bordered on each side by lower wings. The expansive brick front porch was bedecked with four towering white pillars and the mansion's rows of double windows were protected by heavy green shutters. A sweeping gallery roof sloped down over the wings to where it nearly grazed the ground. Out back were the rows of slave cabins, many of which had their doors painted blue to keep out evil spirits.

The master of the plantation was a very old man; his lady was a young vibrant woman named Rose. She loved to entertain lavishly at the great mansion. Guests arrived by paddle wheel steamers that cruised past the El Rio Mansion down the Suwannee River. One particular guest would remain on the premises for weeks at a time. It was rumored among the slaves that Rose had bewitched the handsome young man who became her paramour.

There was a large flower garden behind the mansion that was laid out with walking paths, many benches, and small structures where a person could sit and rest or become romantic with one another. Rose enjoyed this garden, particularly favoring the white roses—even preferring their fragile beauty over the gifts of jewelry her husband lavished on her. It was to the garden that Rose took her paramour. It was here that they walked through the roses under the moonlight and it was here that they shared the love in their hearts.

One of the female slaves knew of these meetings and, probably seeking to gain favor from the master, told Rose's aged husband about them. One night the husband followed Rose and the young man into the garden where he confronted them. He shot the young man to death and had Rose dragged into a room in the mansion which had barred windows where she was left to die of starvation and a broken heart. Before she died, she cursed her husband's family, vowing that she would return each year when the roses were in bloom to take vengeance on members of his family. Rose was buried in the garden beneath the roses she loved so much.

Today, in the misty dusk, Rose's ghost is often seen crossing through the garden toward the old mansion, which is no longer in use. She glides to the doors and shuttered windows and pounds on them in her fury. Perhaps her curse was fulfilled because there is no longer anyone in the old house to be terrified by her. The elderly husband's line has died out. However, it is very likely that while he was still alive Rose's ghost exacted a good deal of vengeance on the old man. Slaves of the plantation told of seeing her ghost in its yearly haunting and that they would hide behind their blue doors until the evil passed away.

CLOCK TOWER SPECTRE

Our ghost hunt continues on the streets of Tallahassee, a city that has gathered its fair share of specters. Tallahassee is the capital of Florida and is located where Highways 10 and 19 come together and is easily reached from anywhere in the state by taking one of these routes.

The ghost in question shuttles between two locations: the clock tower and the cemetery where its moral remains had been laid to rest. The clock tower can be found in downtown Tallahassee on South Macomb Street. It was built in 1910 and was constructed as part of a personal cottage by the well-known architect Calvin C. Phillips.

Mr. Phillips moved to Florida from Pennsylvania where he won an industry award for designing a portable grist mill. It was not long after he arrived in Tallahassee that he began work on his now famous clock tower. It was designed based on those in use in the thirteenth-century England. The illustrious architect chose to reside alone in the cottage beside the clock tower rather than in the same house with his wife. Whether this was because he loved the clock tower so much or hated his wife so deeply is not known to the author.

Clock tower/mausoleum of Calvin Phillips, whose ghost appears here. (*Author's photo.*)

Mr. Phillips also built a well-known burial vault—his own. It is located in Oakland Cemetery in Tallahassee and is the site of the first burial there. His vault is a most grand structure with a twenty-foot-high minaret towering to the sky and an impressive marble plate on the wall.

Calvin Phillips had notable carpentry skills, too. In addition to designing his burial vault, he built his own coffin out of cherrywood and the bier upon which it rested. He must have known that his death was near because he died only a few days after work on his tomb was completed. And he wasn't going to take any chances on being interred anywhere but there. Just before he died, he entered his tomb and gave the keys to the door to a friend instructing him to lock him inside after he had died. His friend did so. This was in 1911 and the tomb has not been disturbed since. The clock tower has not fared as well, having been broken into by vandals. The chimes of the clock no longer operate.

Calvin Phillips' ghost returns occasionally to both of his most beloved properties. Strange sounds and peculiar lights have been reported from the vacant clock tower and similar manifestations have been noted at the burial vault. Maybe the ghost returns to perform periodic maintenance at these two sites or simply to relive pleasant memories of his past life. If only he could get those chimes on the clock to work again.

JAILHOUSE PHANTOMS

Our ghost quest next takes us to the old Leon County Jail. The jail stopped functioning as such in the 1960s but it is still in use as the location where state archives are stored. Since the old jail is now a public building in downtown Tallahassee, you will need to be on some semblance of official business to be on the premises. This jail is one of the most haunted sites in Florida. Not only are there many ghosts here—but they are hostile and malevolent.

Hardened, vicious criminals were kept locked behind these one-foot thick walls of concrete and steel. Escape from here has proven impossible. A number of the desperate inmates committed suicide rather than face the prospect of remaining here. One determined prisoner tried to make his escape by climbing up the shaft of a dumbwaiter but did not make it. His body was found crushed beneath the elevator at the bottom of the shaft.

Numerous skeletons have turned up in various unexpected places throughout this damp old building. During general renovations for more office space in 1966, two skeletons were found in a hidden wall compartment. Later, a knife and two brown beer bottles were discovered in another secret room that was unearthed in the depths of this grim structure.

The old Leon County Court House. Many ghosts from the past were raised here during renovation. (*Author's photo*)

A séance was held to determine if any other strange mysteries lay in wait. The séance was conducted by Patricia Hayes who found the spirits to be of such a violent and evil nature that she concluded the proceedings prematurely. She did have enough time, however, to develop a description of one of the spirits. It matched the description of a former criminal who used to kidnap local vagrants and force them to work on his farm. He abused them and subjected them to all types of cruelty and he himself was eventually brutally murdered.

During the séance, Ms. Hayes was also given the location of one of the many secret rooms in the building by one of the spirits. This information proved to be correct; this was where the knife and beer bottles were found using information supplied by the spirit.

The old Leon County jail is still a dark drafty building despite the remodeling and it retains many of the poorly-lighted stairways and some of the actual cell blocks. Employees who work here in the archives and records center have reported meeting ghostly apparitions in the cold secluded stairwells and feeling their presence around them as they go about their work. Robert Biggs (named changed) remembers encountering a ghost in 1980 while he was storing papers in the state archives vault. Something tapped him on the shoulder and when he turned to se who it was, no one was there.

Steven Lewin (name changed) of Record Management Services often works late at night and on several occasions has heard loud sledgehammer-like pounding on the back wall. There was no construction work being done on the building at that hour nor were any repairs going on in the street outside. Mr. Lewin reported that the noise he heard was so loud and insistent that he expected to find the concrete wall cracked the next morning. It had not even been dented.

Again working late into the night, Mr. Lewin was passing by one of the cell blocks when he was startled to see one of the 100 lb. steel cell doors open, stop, then close by itself. Neither a draft nor a gust of wind could have caused such a heavy door to move like that.

There has not been any shortage of witnesses to the ghostly events that occur on a regular basis at this highly haunted site. Any time a person enters a room he could walk into the specter of a former inmate; any time that someone ventures into one of the gloomy staircases he has a good chance to encounter a ghost.

Perhaps it should not be surprising to have so much activity in a building that has housed such violent and even insane criminals for such a long period of time. Add to this the number of deaths that have occurred here over the years and you have a perfect formula for many a haunting.

There may be even more to come. Have all of the secret rooms been found? Have all of the skeletons in the walls been unearthed? Even if they have, however, there are already enough spirits in the old Leon County Jail to keep everyone on the edge of his or her seat. If you have any official business in the Records Department in Tallahassee, you might find yourself on an unsuspectingly spooky errand— even if it is just to say hello to a ghost.

OLD MAN EPPES

This haunted location is the site of a former plantation just outside of Tallahasee. It is not easily accessible and is in a state of disrepair. The Eppes Plantation was a typical antebellum estate, consisting of a grand pillared home, vast acreage, and a large work force of slaves. After a long weekend of backbreaking work in the fields and drudgery taking care of the Master's house, the slaves would often gather at a central spot on the grounds and have a boisterous jamboree. They brought out the barrels of homemade moonshine and their musical instruments and drank and played music deep into the night.

These weekend parties were usually rowdy affairs, which the White people who lived on the plantations avoided as a rule. One night, however, Old Man Eppes—the owner of the plantation—decided to drop in on the merrymaking. It would have been better for him if he had kept his distance like on the other nights.

While at the jubilation, Mr. Eppes took a fancy to one of the attractive female slaves. He made advances to her and let it be known that he wanted her intimate company. This enraged the female slave's lover, who confronted the plantation owner. A scuffle ensued and then a full-fledged fight. Mr. Eppes was killed. Stunned silence replaced the shouting and the sounds of fist fighting. What to do? The Master lay dead in the field amidst the gathering of slaves.

The only solution that anyone could come up with was to carry Old Man Eppes back to his carriage and drive him back to the mansion. This is what they did, leaving the corpse in the front seat of the carriage, hoping that whoever found the dead man would assume he had simply died there due either to natural causes or an attack from an intruder.

It is not told what kind of punishment was meted out to the man who murdered Mr. Eppes or if his identity was ever uncovered. However, Old Man Eppes makes his return to the old plantation when the moon is full. Not only has he been seen walking the grounds, but witnesses also report hearing the chanting and singing voices of slaves. Other people have seen Mr. Eppes' ghostly carriage rushing up the pathway from the fields toward the mansion, re-enacting the night on which he was spirited home after being killed.

There are many ghosts still walking the grounds of the Eppes Plantation. They are all still bound together by what happened on that tragic night when Old Man Eppes decided to join his slaves in their jamboree—a jamboree that still takes place with the full moon.

A WITCH'S RETURN

This haunting also takes place on the outskirts of Tallahassee in the Old City Cemetery. Elizabeth Budd Graham was born about the year 1886. Her life was a most interesting one involving witchcraft and various occult practices. Elizabeth was an avowed witch, but not of the dark cauldron-stirring variety; she was more modern in her approach to the ancient craft. She chose the light side of witchcraft to engage in and by most accounts she was a gentle likable person who treated others with good will. Yet, she was a witch!

In the last half of the nineteenth century, the general conception of a witch was that of an evil gnarled person who was a mistress of the Devil. It didn't matter that she was young and pretty or that she chose to help

Tallahassee's Old City Cemetery, haunted by illustrious personages from the past. (*Author's photo*)

people and encourage the pursuit of spiritual goals; she was a witch and witches were bad.

When she was in her early twenties, Elizabeth married a wealthy man. Most people believed that she had bewitched him into the marriage, as if being pretty, intelligent, and kind-hearted were not enough charms to win a man's heart. Elizabeth gave birth to a child soon after the marriage, but the good witch died two years later at the age of twenty-three of unspecified causes.

According to her Wiccan beliefs, Elizabeth's grave in the Old City Cemetery is facing west as opposed to Christian tradition. Upon her monument is inscribed an epitaph that has spellbound many who have visited this haunted grave and read the fateful message.

Ah! Broken is the golden bowl,
The spirit flown forever!
Let the bell toll! A saintly
Soul flows on the Stygian river;
Come let the burial rite be read,
The funeral song be sung; an anthem
For the queenliest dead that ever
Died so young. A dirge for her the
Doubly dead in that she died so
Young.

The spirit of Elizabeth Budd Graham has been often seen hovering over this grave site. Many people visit the location of her burial and one person in particular has paid her respects on an almost daily basis. Her identity is not known. Could she perhaps be a granddaughter or another relative? Perhaps she is a devout believer in witchcraft and venerates Elizabeth as a saint. Or could this mysterious visitor be Elizabeth herself? Even in death the enigma of this good witch persists. And still she has harmed no one and offers words for meditation and a place of peace.

THE BEDSIDE SPECTER

This story dates back to December 15, 1907, where it appeared as a true Christmas ghost story in the *Pensacola Journal*. It concerns a former officer of the French Navy named Jarlier who, upon retiring, moved with his French Creole wife into a modest but fine home in Pensacola.

Although Jarlier was older than his wife, he was in excellent health when he moved into the home on Baylen Street and was by all accounts a handsome man of good character. His health began to fail him, however, and it was on Christmas Eve in 1906 that his wife told some friends who had stopped by for the holidays that she had seen a ghost of ill-omen and was extremely troubled.

Mrs. Jarlier had been sitting at her now-ailing, though still spirited, husband's bedside the day before Christmas Even when the frightening vision occurred. A beautiful female ghost dressed in white appeared at the head of Mr. Jarlier's bed as he slept, ruefully wringing her hands, and sobbing aloud that the poor man would be dead in only two months time. The ghost then vanished as suddenly as she had appeared.

Mrs. Jarlier hurried to her husband's side but found that he was still peacefully asleep. The room had become chilled with the deepening night, so Mrs. Jarlier placed more wood on the fire before returning to her seat at the foot of the bed. Despite the growing blaze, the room got even colder. That is when she noted the return of the spectral intruder. Once again the ghost stood beside Mr. Jarlier, made her tearful prediction, then disappeared.

Mrs. Jarlier rushed to her husband again and found him still in a sound sleep. Kneeling, the woman said some prayers, and returned to her seat. Not long afterward, the ghost made her third appearance and again repeated her prophecy before vanishing. This time the terrified woman awoke her husband and told him what she had seen and heard. Not overly concerned, Jarlier told his wife that she had probably been dreaming and that she should come to bed.

The friends to whom Mrs. Jarlier told this story attempted to comfort her but to little avail. During the following days, Mr. Jarlier's health steadily worsened. When the friends who had visited on Christmas Eve made another visit at the end of February, they were informed that Mr. Jarlier had died on February 23, exactly when the ghost had predicted.

THE PHANTOM PATROL

During the War Between the States, both the Southern and Northern forces regularly patrolled the Yellow River, which was just south of the Alabama-Florida state line. A Confederate regiment known as the Walton Guards was station at East Pass, where they stood on the lookout for Northern blockade schooners. Two of these ships— the *U.S.S. Charlotte* and the *U.S.S. Marie*—frequently dispatched foraging parties to the shore to ravage the Southern countryside for food and supplies.

The Confederates made contact with one of these foraging parties and engage it in a fierce but brief battle. A number of Union soldiers were killed in the skirmish and their bodies were taken to Old Bethel Cemetery for burial, near the town of Crestview. The soldiers, who remain unidentified to this day, were placed in graves marked only with square stones.

The uneasy spirits of these Union soldiers still roam the ground upon which they were killed. Since the location of the battle is deep in the countryside, the sightings of the ghostly patrol are mostly made by hunters or hikers who are the only ones to venture out there. But many have seen the patrol. The sighting is always the same: a troubled-faced Union officer leads his small mounted band around the bend in the Yellow River and then back into oblivion. It seems that the enlistment period for these Union soldiers may extend into eternity.

NORTH EAST COAST
JACKSONVILLE--
ST. AUGUSTINE AREA

JACKSONVILLE HAUNTS

Jacksonville is a large metropolis on the northeastern corner of Florida. There are a number of vintage old buildings that look out on the Bay and it seems that the spirits of their former occupants have remained tied to this picturesque location. In the Mayport area is a tall drafty old building known as the King House. It is still the home of several spirits. One of them is William Joseph King—a gnarled stubby-bearded seaman from the early 1800s.

William King came to the Jacksonville area from Delaware, having worked for a time as a cook on a schooner. He met sixteen-year-old Clara Arnau and promptly married her. Clara's father was a wealthy bar owner and when he died William King took over both the bar and his father-in-law's mansion. Today, the ghost of the elderly William King is often seen peering down from the mansion's long flight of stairs. Witnesses have also heard the loud voices of several boisterous women from the balcony to which the staircase leads. The noisy group has also been seen, but the identity of these women is still a mystery—perhaps just as well taking into account their behavior.

A grim story arises from one of the dark homes in extreme northeastern Jacksonville. Anna, a plain very hard-working woman, lived in the Tallyrand House with her husband and two children. One day, the two children walked in on their reprobate father while he was in the midst of having sex with a strange woman. Flying from bed in a fit, the homewrecking woman chased the two children and killed both of them. Anna walked into the horrific scene and fell into a fierce battle with the other woman, which ended with Anna being stabbed to death. Fleeing madly from the room, the other woman knocked over a lantern, which crashed to the floor and sent a trail of flames rushing down the hall. Anna's house was quickly engulfed in fire—as was the woman who had started it. Since that time, two houses have been built on this location and both have been haunted by the ghost of Anna, for whom time has not passed at this site of terrible tragedy.

A large cast of characters haunts a grand house on Magnolia Street in Green Cove Springs. The building is now a family residence, but at one time it was a boarding house which accounts for the number of spirits who have remained here and their family-like interest in those who currently occupy the structure.

As one of the more recent owners of the Green Cove Springs house was doing repairs in the attic he arose from his work to find that a curious old ghost had been standing behind him, peeping over his shoulder. The elderly spirit was dressed in gray work clothes and had the manners to excuse himself before vanishing. On another occasion, this same owner of the house saw an elderly woman sitting at the edge of his bed, watching him. The air suddenly became alive with faint music arising from a spectral Victrola.

While more remodeling was being done to the historic building, a baby's coffin was discovered in a space between the ceiling and the attic in one of the bedrooms. Since then, the sound of a baby's crying has been heard coming from this room. Prior to the discovery of the coffin, anyone who stayed in this cursed bedroom went through a drastic personality change, becoming suddenly hostile and argumentative.

On one occasion, the wife of one of the modern-day owners of the house glimpsed a teenage girl in old-fashioned clothing fleeting down one of the hallways. It could not have been the owner's daughter because she was not home at the time. Her daughter, however, was to have an unusual experience herself. One day while she was ascending the stairs she placed her hand upon the railing only to feel something that felt like another hand under hers. It was the wrinkled powdery-white hand of an elderly woman.

Another odd phenomenon that occurs at this Green Cove Springs home is the sudden appearance of a ball of light, which would either spring out of the fireplace or from the shadows to startle unsuspecting witnesses. Many of the ghosts who appear here do so at times when remodeling is being performed or when guests are visiting. It is as if many of the former occupants are still on hand and very interested in the goings-on of the household. To them, it seems, the building is still just one big boarding house where everybody knew everybody else's business. Even ghosts can be busybodies at times.

FRIGHTENING ST. AUGUSTINE

Ponce de Leon was searching for the fountain of youth when he landed in Florida in 1513. He claimed the land for Spain and it remained a Spanish possession until 1821 except for a brief twenty-year span when England ruled it from 1763 to 1783.

The French staked a claim in Florida, too, and in 1564 settled a colony near the St. John's River. The Spanish did not approve of this and the next year Admiral Pedro Menendez destroyed the fledgling French outpost. He renamed this site St. Augustine after the famous church father and Bishop of Hippo.

One of the oldest cities in the United States, St. Augustine has had a great deal of time to acquire an impressive list of ghosts and haunted places.

A TYCOON'S GHOST

One of the city's most well-known spirits belongs to that of the tycoon Henry Flagler. Flagler first visited St. Augustine in 1884 while honeymooning with his second wife, Alice. The wealthy railroad magnate and partner of John D. Rockefeller, Sr. was much impressed with the area, especially its moneymaking potential as a resort haven for the elite. Thus, in 1885, Henry Flagler returned to St. Augustine to remain with the intention of developing a resort for the rich and powerful. Mr. Flagler built many hotels in Florida including the Ponce de Leon, the Alcazar, and the Cordova. The Ponce de Leon later became Flagler College, while the Alcazar is now the Lightner Museum. The Cordova was turned into a government office building.

Henry Morrison Flagler. (*Author's photo*)

Henry Flagler died while visiting friends in Palm Beach on May 20, 1913, and his body was returned to St. Augustine where it lay in state in the rotunda of the Ponce de Leon. The ghost of Mr. Flagler wasted no time in announcing its presence and also in leaving an indelible impression behind. When the funeral cortège arrived to remove Mr. Flagler's body from the rotunda for burial, the huge doors slammed closed loudly behind them by themselves. The assembled were frozen in shock. When their nerves steadied, someone found the strength to approach the doors and open them so that the body of the late tycoon could be carried out in procession. The spirit had left something behind, however. Decorating the rotunda floor is an impressive design of tiles. If a person investigates the tiles closely, a dime-sized impression of the likeness of Henry Flagler that appeared there after his death can be seen. The impression is still there today.

Flagler College, where Henry Flagler and his wife's ghost still walk.
(*Author's photo*)

In 1968, the Ponce de Leon was converted into Flagler College, a small liberal arts school of high quality. The ghosts of Henry Flagler, his second wife, and his mistress haunt this building of higher education. Alice Flagler was an energetic, pretty, wildly eccentric strawberry blonde. After a life of indulgence and extravagance, she eventually declined into insanity and was placed in an asylum where she died raving at the walls.

The mansion of Henry Flagler, known as Whitehall. Ghosts have been seen there. (*Author's photo*)

Today her ghost is often seen in the coed's dormitory of the College. A ghostly apparition fitting her description has been seen walking the halls and standing at the end of a bed, peering quietly down at the person who happens to be sleeping there that night. Her face has occasionally appeared on dormitory doors. Obviously, Mrs. Flagler has chosen to stay at the hotel.

Perhaps Mrs. Flagler has remained to keep watch for the ghost of her late husband's mistress. The mistress lived at the Ponce de Leon. On one occasion, Mrs. Flagler came to the hotel for a lengthy stay and in order to avoid trouble, Mr. Flagler exiled his mistress to a room at the far end of the building to keep the two women from meeting. The mistress could not tolerate this situation and eventually hung herself in despair. Hers is the ghost in black who makes appearances on the top floor of the west wing. Apparently, she and Mrs. Flagler have not met in the afterlife either.

Flagler College is a school that has given a special meaning to the concept of a well-rounded education. Maybe 'Haunting 101' should be added to the curriculum.

VISIONS IN THE WILDWOOD

A strange visitor comes to the Wildwood Baptist Church whenever the hymn *Zion's Hill* is sung. As the lyrics rise to heaven, as if to summon ghostly worshippers, the form of a man dressed in a black suit and wearing a top hat enters from a back door and quietly takes his seat in the minister's chair. He remains there, silent and at peace, until the hymn is completed—then he simply vanishes.

Many have seen him. He is such a common sight that only newcomers to the church are surprised by his presence. The apparition belongs to Mr. Anthony, a former parishioner, who had died many years ago. *Zion's Hill* was his favorite hymn—and apparently still is.

Odd things have happened in the Wildwood churchyard, too. One day at dusk, a man walked past the cemetery and noticed a stone statue of an angel about six feet tall standing alongside a fresh grave at neither the head nor the foot of the new burial mound—but at its midpoint. A peculiar spot for a statue! Even more peculiar was what the man saw—or did not see—early the next morning when he made his way back past the graveyard. The statue of the angel was gone!

Along with the disappearing angel, the churchyard also has a rather boisterous tenant buried there. On one occasion, a couple of women wound their way through the historic cemetery, taking information from the headstones for a genealogical study. A few nights later, after the project was finished, one of the women was startled from her sleep by a ghostly shout: "You forgot the one in the middle!"

Associating this cry with her just finished genealogical study and assuming that the call was from the occupant of an overlooked grave, the woman took her friend back to the churchyard the next day to appease the spirit. After hours of fruitless searching for a headstone that they had missed in earlier tours of the grounds, the woman accidentally uncovered an area of moss that had been smothering a ground-level headstone. It belonged to Henry O'Barnum (1828-1880)—the one in the middle.

THE PERFUMED WALL

The Castillo de San Marcos was built by the Spanish in 1672 and is the oldest fort still standing in the United States. In 1784, Colonel Garcia Marti was in command of the Fort when Spain regained control over the Florida Territory after twenty years of British rule.

Colonel Marti had a beautiful young wife who was a faithful type. The Colonel also had a subordinate officer, Captain Manuel Abela, who was not a trustworthy type. A clandestine romance developed between Señora Marti and Captain Abela. It was not easy to keep their affair from becoming known and becoming the main topic of gossip in the small community. Finally, the Colonel heard the rumors.

Colonel Marti had a plan to find out if the stories were true. One night he told his wife that he had a meeting with Governor Zespedes and that he would return later. Then the Colonel hid in a concealed place in their house to await what would transpire, if anything. His wife eagerly contacted her lover who quickly came to her. While they were heedlessly enjoying each other's company, Colonel Marti broke in upon them from his place of hiding and probably would have killed both of them instantly if he had not been stopped from doing so by a friend of his.

Castillo de San Marcos where a spectral scent of perfume clings to the dungeon walls. (*Author's photo*)

The Colonel ordered that his wife and her lover be chained to the Castillo's dungeon wall. A short time later, having grown angrier and angrier over the betrayal, he commanded the entrance to the cell where the two were chained up to be walled over. Here is where the two lovers died.

In 1833, construction work was being undertaken on the Castillo de San Marcos. When a workman broke through the wall that covered the dungeon cell where the two lovers had been confined, he was overwhelmed by the intense aroma of perfume. Inside the cell were the skeletons of the two lovers, hanging on the wall—still in chains.

Witnesses today claim to have seen an eerie glow come from the dungeon and to be able to smell perfume wafting from the wall where the pretty, but unfaithful, señorita had hung.

A LIGHT FROM THE CASABLANCA

The Casablanca is now a popular bread-and-breakfast located at 24 Avenida Menendez. It was built in 1914 and in its former incarnation—before restoration, that is—it was a boarding house.

During the Prohibition Era, St. Augustine was a crucial port for smuggling in liquor from Jamaica, Puerto Rico, and Cuba. This harbor was not as closely guarded by Treasury agents as others along the east coast of Florida. The Casablanca Inn was strategically located along the shore of the Mantanzas Bay—a perfect landing spot for smugglers. An elderly lady owned the boarding house during the 1920s and 1930s where many traveling salesmen as well as Treasury agents stopped for the night, or longer, under her roof.

Being an enterprising woman, the elderly lady knew that it would be valuable for the liquor smugglers to know when the Treasury agents were in town, so she offered to supply them with this information for a fee. A deal was struck. Whenever it was safe to bring in an illegal shipment of liquor, the woman would climb to the widow's walk of the Casablanca and signal with a lantern.

Her lookout activities continued until Prohibition was repealed, but by that time she had become a millionaire. When she died, she was buried in the historic Huguenot Cemetery. Her ghost, however, is still signaling out to sea from the renovated widow's walk of the Casablanca Inn. Instead of being seen by smugglers, the light of her lantern is now being seen by shrimpers, fisherman, and pleasure boaters. Then again . . . maybe there is a ghostly smuggler ship or two still out there.

GHOSTS OF CATALINA GARDENS

The following account is about a haunted restaurant in St. Augustine. One particularly interesting feature of the story is the similarity between this location and the haunted restaurant at Rockledge. Both have haunted ladies' rooms.

The Catalina Gardens was, for most of its history, used as private residences and only later was converted into a dining establishment. The original structure was built in 1745 for Juana and Francisco de Porras, who eventually had nine children. The youngest child was named Catalina. When England took possession of Florida for twenty years, Catalina and her family relocated to Cuba. Only Catalina ever returned to Florida—with her husband—in 1784. Unfortunately, Catalina only had a short time to enjoy her childhood home because she died only six years after moving back into the house.

In 1887, a great fire swept through St. Augustine and among the many buildings that were destroyed was Catalina's home. However, relying on sketches drawn by John Horton, the structure was rebuilt a year later in its original location. It remained a private residence until 1976 when it was converted into a restaurant at 46 Avenida Menendez.

One of the first encounters with paranormal activity was made by members of the night cleaning crew. It occurred in the upstairs ladies' room where the figure of a woman in a long white dress was glimpsed briefly before vanishing. It is believed to be the apparition of Catalina and has been seen repeatedly throughout the building. One of the day cleaning crew also noticed something very strange about the upstairs ladies' room. It is often bathed in the deep aroma of heady perfume of an unearthly nature, a common occurrence that has been experienced by a great many people.

Another sighting of the woman in white was made near the first floor patio doors. Here, early in the morning, one of the employees saw the woman in the long white dress standing at the door, jiggling its handle. The witness viewed the full face of the ghost before the specter vanished. The ghost has also been spotted by the owner of the restaurant in his third floor office. On one occasion while working late at night he felt a presence quickly flit behind his chair. The presence rushed toward the copy machine before disappearing. No one else was in the building at the time.

Lights in the building have come on by themselves numerous times. Even more eerie is that the table top candles have also lighted themselves, as has the main room fireplace. On the second floor of the restaurant is a waiter's station where a mirror hangs. On at least one occasion, the reflection of a woman in white has been seen in this mirror.

One psychic who visited the site believes that the room with the fireplace was Catalina's bedroom and that her spirit is restless because of the difficulties the woman had had with a man during her physical life on earth.

There is also a male ghost known to haunt the restaurant. He wears an old-fashioned suit from the early 1900s and has been seen descending the stairway the leads to the wine case. Some believe that this is the spirit of a person who died in the fire of 1887. However, a more likely possibility is that the entity belongs to an elderly man who was sent by his doctor to live in Florida as a way to get relief from his poor health. In addition to this, the great grand-daughter of the alleged ghost has stated that her great grandfather had indeed spent time at this location just before he died of his illness.

Encounters with Catalina and the mysterious man in the old-fashioned suit take place in the day. The Catalina Gardens would seem to be an ideal spot for a ghost hunter. Not only will the friendly staff here serve you a fine dinner, but they will most likely add a ghost story or two for dessert.

KIXIE'S PHANTOMS

In the mid-1940s, Kixie's Men's Store was located at 28 St. George Street in St. Augustine. Kenny Beeson worked there as the tailor. His workroom in the back of the store was large and comfortable and Kenny spent many late nights there running the sewing machines and performing all the other tasks of his profession.

One night, while working late and alone, Kenny was startled from hemming a pair of pants by the sound of a doorknob turning. He peered in that direction and, in amazement, watched as the knob turned and the door opened by itself! An overwhelming aroma of intensely sweet funeral flowers poured over him and refused to dissipate. Kenny was so sickened by the deep fragrance that he put down his work, closed the shop and fled. When he reached his house, the odor of flowers was still quite potent although his wife could not smell it.

From that day on, Kenny was frequently visited at the shop by the presence. He would know of its whereabouts by the opening and closing of doors by themselves and the moving of objects from one place to another in the workroom. And there was always that ever-present aroma of funeral flowers which no else could detect.

Then the pace of the ghostly events accelerated. A new phenomena commenced: the sound of footsteps marching in rhythm on wood flooring. There were no wooden floors in the building. The cadence was like that of sailors marching on the deck of a ship. Others heard the marching as well: Preston Lay became the first person other than Kenny to experience the nauseating odor.   After more unusual occurrences took place that night, Kenny decided to leave with his friend Mr. Lay. Before leaving, however, Kenny put a blank tape into a small tape recorder and started it running. He closed all the doors and securely locked the building before departing.

The next day, Kenny returned to the shop to find the interior doors that he had locked were now wide open. He retrieved his tape recorder, rewound the tape, and turned it on. The sounds of he and his friend leaving the workroom and driving away were distinctly recorded. So were the sounds made by nocturnal spectral visitors! There was the thumping of doors opening and closing, the stomping of footsteps marching on an unseen wooden floor, and some frightening guttural sounds that were not made by a living being. There was also assorted scratching and squeaking made by unknown creatures.

Kenny had had enough and contacted Monsignor Harold Jordan for the purpose of performing an exorcism. The priest agreed to undertake the rite and proceeded to bless the store and exhort the evil spirits to depart. From that time onward, the phenomena ceased— all except one. The sickening sweet odor of funeral flowers continued to smother the workshop. No one ever discovered the cause of this scent or why it still clung to the interior of the building.

CENTRAL FLORIDA

MA BARKER AND FRIENDS

Gangster-type ghosts are rare in Florida. As already noted, people usually come here in their later years to retire and live a peaceful life. Even Ma Barker and her friends came down here to relax from their nefarious activities—before their vacation was suddenly cut short by the FBI.

Ma Barker was born in 1897 near Springfield, Missouri. Her maiden name was Clark. She was more commonly known in the earlier days of her profession as 'Arizona Donnie' Barker. When she was still quite young, Arizona Donnie married George Barker with whom she managed to sire—it is believed—four sons. The sons—criminals all—were, according to age: Herman 'Bloody' Barker (1894-1927), Lloyd Barker (1896-1949), Arthur 'Doc' Barker (1899-1939), and Fred Barker (1902-1935). Oddly enough, George Barker did not have a criminal record.

After Ma Barker left her husband she got together with her sons and a few of their friends and swept across the Midwest from Minnesota to Texas on a crime spree that lasted from the mid-1920s to the mid-1930s. As the matriarch of the gang, Ma directed the kidnappings, payroll heists, and bank and post office robberies. In their wake they left many dead police officers.

Needing to take a much-needed break from the routine of stealing and killing, Ma led her gang down to a resort in Florida near Ocala. They found a spacious two-story building in which to stay in Ocklawaha overlooking Lake Weir. To visit this location, proceed south from Ocala on Highway 301, turn east on Highway 464 until you reach the small town of Ocklawaha. Any one of the nine hundred or so citizens who live there can direct you there. In fact, you may be able to rent a room at this very haunted site.

In the mid-1930s, the FBI was beginning a serious crackdown on 'public enemies.' They claimed to have shot John Dillinger dead one July night in 1934 outside of the Biograph Theater in Chicago. However, autopsy records released thirty years later prove that another man

Grandmotherly Ma Barker
with date Arthur V. Dunlop.
(*Archives*)

was really shot that night and has left his ghost at that site. Bonnie and
Clyde, 'Pretty Boy' Floyd, 'Baby Face' Nelson and many others had
been chased down and bumped off—or were about to be. Maybe Ma
Barker and her group thought that they were safe holed up in Florida,
which back in the 1930s was mostly swamp and alligator country.

Ma Barker and her shady group spent their time drinking, playing cards, and fighting among themselves. With all the booze they
drank and the food they ate, they were probably an economic boon to
this tiny community. They were certainly the ranking celebrities of
the time.

One day in January, 1935, however, their vacation came to an abrupt end. The FBI had surrounded the entire building with an arsenal of weapons and Ma Barker and her clan were called back to work. What ensued was the longest FBI shoot out of all time. A steady battery of machine gun fire sprayed the building. The occasional blast of a shotgun was hardly heard amidst the constant, unrelenting chattering of the machine guns. Bullets tore through the wooden walls of the house, tearing the siding to shreds.

The Oklawaha retreat where Ma Barker and her clan
were slain. (*Author's photo*)

The interior didn't fare any better. There was barely a spot of wall that had not been dug out by a machine gun round. The old-fashioned wooden furniture was chewed to splinters by the non-stop gunfire. The floor was littered with shards of glass from the blown-out windows, fragments of window-dressing were strewn everywhere and the remains of the table and chairs slumped in contorted positions, missing arms and legs. And amidst it all were Ma Barker and Fred, firing, reloading, and firing again.

Nothing could be heard above the horrific sound of gunfire. Most of the FBI agents were wearing earplugs and couldn't hear anything anyway. They didn't even know if they were still being fired upon. It didn't matter. The strategy was to maintain a continual barrage of gunfire until it was determined that no one inside the house could possibly be still left alive. It was almost as if the house itself were being killed.

Finally, with a wave of his arm, the FBI agent-in-charge signaled a halt to the attack. A stunned silence ensued. The entire landscape was frozen; all of the wildlife had fled and it seemed that even nearby Lake Wier was frozen in shock. However, the house that had been the target of the assault was still going through its death throes. Eventually, the sound of raining plaster, pictures falling off the walls and furniture at last succumbing could be heard through the quiet. Ma Barker and her son, Fred, were dead, riddled with bullet holes as they lay amidst the debris of the house.

When the FBI agents marched into the house, even they were taken aback by the extent of the devastation they had inflicted. More

Aftermath of the Ma Barker shootout. *(Archives photo)*

astonishing than what was destroyed, however, was what had been left undamaged. Still hanging from the ceiling—untouched—was the chandelier and leaning back in the corner of one of the walls was a china cabinet, also not nicked by a single bullet.

Both Ma Barker and Fred were promptly put on display, full of bullet holes, like hunting trophies. The house where they had been killed was eventually repaired and re-rented. Apparently, however, Ma Barker and her friends still like it there because they are back— as spirits. The house on Lake Weir is busy with ghostly activity. It is almost as if Ma Barker and her gang had never left. Footsteps and voices can be heard coming from all over the building. Especially active is the main room where Ma and her cohorts spent a lot of their time. The sound of an ongoing card game is so loud that witnesses are able to hear the cards slapping down onto the table top and chips being flipped and thrown.

Ghostly fighting can still be heard as well. Loud voices are often heard from the upstairs room; one can almost decipher what is being said. It seems like the 'good old days' are being played over and over and over again for Ma Barker and her gang. They came here for a vacation and it seems like this one will never end.

Ironically, sounds of the gun battle have not been widely reported. Maybe in the afterlife, Ma and the boys have outwitted the G-men who furnished them with a permanent vacation. Tourists are welcome here and if you like you can drop by the small town of Ocklawaha and visit Ma Barker and her clan and have a taste of southern hospitality.

SPIRITS OF THE KISSIMMEE RIVER

During the last part of the nineteenth and early part of the twentieth century, Kissimmee River was heavily traveled between Lake Kissimmee and Lake Okeechobee. It was the watery thoroughfare by which goods and people were transported through the heart of

Florida. Kissimmee River winds through dense sub-tropical vegetation and vast areas of unpopulated land. At night, the dark along the shores is unbroken and intense; overhead the hazy stream of the Milk Way spans the black sky. A wilderness could not be more complete—or more haunting.

Along the Kissimmee River are many hidden inlets and small bays. A few such inlets have become notable for being haunted. Ben Yates, an old-time river pilot, had occasion to pass by many of these secluded inlets and recounts various tales of strange sights and sounds. One hidden bay in particular is notorious for weird phenomena. Even in the daylight, it is a haunting place where trees reach out over the water as if to attack any who intrude on its solitude. The quiet here is unnerving and unnatural; the waters of the bay are motionless and dead. There is always a gloomy darkness because of the grappling overhanging branches.

There are times, however, when the stillness of the inlet is violently disturbed. Ben Yates notes that on several occasions he was drawn over to the usually quiet bay by the sound of the water being violently thrashed. Upon detouring to the inlet, he would find the water churning without any apparent cause. Then came the ghostly groans from the nearby trees and the shadowy figures flitting through the gnarled treetops.

There has not been any explanation for the haunting of the secluded bay. Maybe it was the scene of a deadly fight among privateers or maybe it was where an unfortunate person lost his life to a voracious alligator. Whatever the cause of the haunting, it seems to have originated from a particularly violent incident, judging from the splashing of the water and the pain in the groaning voices.

Others besides Ben Yates have been drawn to this disturbed location and report the same type of phenomena. Just recently it was discovered that the ghostly manifestations have extended onto the adjoining land as well. People who have camped in the area report hearing frightening groaning sounds near the River. They would go to investigate and find nothing, but when they returned to their campsite they discovered that their gear had been flung all about the ground by some unseen force.

If you should ever find yourself boating down the Kissimmee River, you should be particularly vigilant while passing that stretch of cypress swamp between the Avon Park Air Force Range and the town of Basinger. And if you should suddenly hear the sound of water being wildly thrashed in one of the secluded inlets, be advised that if you detour to the area you may come across one of Florida's most beguiling unnatural sights.

THE GHOST-FILLED RESTAURANT

The town of Rockledge is on the east coast of Florida on Highway 1. Rockledge is the site of Ashley's Restaurant, which is located at 1609 South U.S. Route 1, not far from Cape Canaveral. Ashley's Restaurant is a two-story Tudor building which was built in the late 1920s. Over the years, it has been known by several names including: the 'Loose Caboose,' the 'Mad Duchess,' and 'Gentleman Jim's.' Ownership has changed hands many times, which some people attribute to the annoying ghostly manifestations. However, the restaurant business is unusually perilous in Florida and the reason for the frequent of owners can also be blamed on this economic fact.

Ashley's is a very haunted site, beset with many odd and verifiable manifestations. One of the most haunted areas in the restaurant is the ladies' room. One witness to the ghostly presence here is the manager who, on one occasion, after closing went to the ladies' room and while seated in her stall noticed in the opening between her stall and the one next to hers a pair of legs and feet. Whoever this stranger was, she was wearing high-heeled high-buttoned boots that were typical of another time. When the manager left her stall to check the one with the stranger in it she found it vacant. Yet she had neither heard nor seen anyone leave.

Lake many ladies' rooms, this one has a double door system where the two doors are separated by a small hallway. After leaving the lobby of the restaurant and entering this hallway to the ladies' room, many of the staff members and patrons have suffered strong choking sensations. On one occasion, a person was actually trapped by some weird force in the narrow hallway and was able to leave only when the door to the restaurant lobby was thrust open by an unseen hand.

Several women have testified to seeing the face of a young woman in 1920s garb staring back at them from the ladies' room mirror and to being startled by water rushing from the faucet of the sink of its own accord.

Another haunted location in the restaurant is on a stairway that leads to the second-floor dining area. Many people have complained about being shoved or rudely bumped by some unseen presence while on these steps.

Whispering voices can often be heard in various places throughout the restaurant in the quiet hours after closing. One psychic investigator brought a tape recorder to the scene and claims to have captured these voices on tape and also to have picked up a sinister buzzing noise on the stairway where people have complained of being shoved.

The local police provide some of the best evidence as to the hauntedness of the restaurant. They often use the parking lot during the night and have noted burglar alarms being triggered with no physical cause and have witnessed lights going on and off by themselves inside the building. They have even reported hearing the sound of a piercing female scream coming from the dark locked restaurant.

Who are the spirits inhabiting this building and why are they still infesting it? It seems clear that one of the spirits belongs to a young woman who was named Ethel Allen who lived in the area in the 1920s. According to psychic impressions, she was murdered at a location not far from the haunted restaurant. She was chased down the stairs by a man with a knife who eventually caught up with her and finished his brutal act. The badly-beaten body of Ethel Allen was found by police on the banks of nearby Indian River.

There is another manifestation that may also account for the haunted stairway. A second psychic saw a violent event in which a man was savagely dragged down the flight of stairs by police officers while his teenage daughters watched in horror. Could this be the cause of the shoving and bumping that so many people have felt as they use this same staircase? Or is it a combination of the two acts that took place here that is still affecting people today?

A local newspaper photographer, who was covering the ghost stories at the restaurant, reports some strange exposures made by his equipment. In one of them, the figure of a man appeared in one of the rooms where there had been no one else present at the time the picture was taken. It is speculated that the form is that of an elderly man who did odd jobs at the restaurant and who lived for a time in one of the spare rooms upstairs.

There is yet another spirit which frequents this location—that of a six-year-old girl. She was killed in an automobile accident on the highway near the restaurant and has been 'felt' inside the building, perhaps having psychically gone there for aid. There are many similarities between this haunted restaurant and one in the Chicago suburb that I have researched. The Chicago restaurant is called the 'Country House' and is located in Clarendon Hills. This site is also troubled by a ghostly staircase which is near the washrooms and by another spirit, which apparently has come to this eatery as a place of refuge. The stairway at the Country House is a very narrow flight which leads to the upper storage rooms and offices. While climbing these steps, a person is overcome by an intense feeling of anxiety that mounts as one nears the top. Psychic readings have shown that a woman had hung herself in the room at the top of the stairs.

But a more striking similarity between the Country House and Ashley's is the visiting child's ghost. One of the spirits at the County House is assumed to belong to a child who was killed in an automobile accident that occurred a short distance down the street shortly after she and her mother had stopped in at the restaurant. An odd coincidence? There are many such coincidences in the world of the paranormal. Some of them seem even stranger than the haunting itself.

SPOOK HILL

Spook Hill is located in Lake Wales, which is almost exactly in the center of the state and can be reached from Tampa by taking Highway 60 east. If traveling from the north or the south, Highway 27 will take you to Lake Wales.

At first, Spook Hill seems to be more of an oddity than anything else. What makes this location so unusual is that if you park your car at the bottom of this mysterious hill and leave the car in neutral, the vehicle will begin to climb up the hill on its own! It is a well-known

Spook Hill where the ghosts take the wheel. (*Author's photo*)

tourist attraction and there is even a white line painted at the spot where you are supposed to park your car in order to experience this unusual phenomenon.

At first, Spook Hill seems to be merely a curiosity or an odd quirk of physics. But it seems a little more substantial as a truly weird phenomenon when compared with a similar location in a small town in Texas where a tragedy occurred during the mid-twentieth century at a badly marked railroad crossing. A school bus full of children was struck and demolished by a fast-moving train one grim afternoon. Since then the location has been haunted.

If you leave your vehicle standing in neutral at the railroad crossing, ghostly presences push the vehicle UP the incline over the tracks and DOWN the other side. In tests that have been performed at this location, baby powder was sprinkled on the back of a car to check for any telltale prints that might be left by unseen entities. The vehicle was mysteriously pushed by some unseen force across the tracks and when the back of the car was examined, not only fingerprints were found impressed in the baby powder but shoe prints as well!

Spook Hill is Lake Wales does not have any known history of tragic occurrences but the similarity with the phenomenon in the small town in Texas is difficult to overlook. Maybe there's a ghostly force in Lake Wales looking out for the safety of anyone who drives near Spook Hill. Maybe it is more dangerous here than anyone has imagined.

THE CITY FOUNDED BY A GHOST

Cassadaga is located in the interior of Florida off of Highway 4 near Deland. To get there take the Lake Helen Exit and proceed west until you reach Cassadaga. If you are looking for spirits you will not be disappointed here. Cassadaga is one of the largest Spiritualist communities in the country. Séances are routinely held in almost every house in this small town, which during the tourist season is overrun by visitors. If you ever do visit here be very respectful to the citizens because Spiritualism is a very sincere belief. The inhabitants here did not 'take up' Spiritualism to attract tourists.

The founding of Cassadaga is in itself a ghost story because in a very real sense this community was discovered through the assistance of a spirit. In the 1880s, George Colby, a devout Spiritualist, went in search of a location at which to settle a Spiritualist community. He was led by a spirit guide named Cassadaga—a Native American spirit—to the position where the present-day city now stands. A large stone monument marks the location to where Mr. Colby was led and the spot at which he duly established a Spiritualist community—one that is still thriving. In a sense, most of the houses here can be said to be haunted due to the very nature of the town since the frequent séances attract spirits on a regular basis.

You can visit Cassadaga any time because it is a city like any other but do not expect a lot of hocus-pocus. Spiritualism is a religious belief and the people who live here treat it as such.

A PIRATE'S SPECTER

Jean Lafitte and his brother, Pierre, came to the United States about the year 1810. They operated a blacksmith shop in New Orleans, which was really a front for their smuggling escapades. Jean directed a smuggling operation from nearby Grande Terre Island, an island he shared with a pirate named Grambo. An argument erupted between the two men as to who should be the leader of the pirate forces—a dispute which Jean settled by killing Grambo.

The Lafitte brothers then proceeded to prey on Spanish ships and slave traders that entered the Gulf of Mexico. During the War of 1812, the Lafittes offered their services to the United States military commander, Andrew Jackson. Because of their vital assistance, the American forces won the pivotal Battle of New Orleans. After the War of 1812, the Lafittes resumed the pirate activities, using the Florida coast primarily as a natural repository for their treasures. One such location was on Seahorse Key, which is a small island in the Cedar Key chain off Florida's west coast.

Jean Lafitte entrusted care of the treasure he buried on Seahorse Key to a long-time friend, Pierre LeBlanc. So that LeBlanc's rounds of the deserted island would be easier and more pleasant, Lafitte left him in possession of a beautiful long-legged Palomino.

Like most places in Florida, Seahorse Key was infested with snakes. One day a snake hunter arrived on the island and was promptly confronted by LeBlanc. The snake hunter convinced him that he was only there to catch varmints and developed a friendship with LeBlanc. Sometime later, however, the snake hunter tricked LeBlanc into getting drunk while remaining sober himself. He followed LeBlanc unobserved when the pirate mounted his Palomino for his nightly rounds. When LeBlanc reached the location of the buried treasure he passed out. The snake hunter did not delay in unearthing the chest.

When LeBlanc regained consciousness and saw what the snake hunter was up to, he drew out his sword and staggered toward the snake hunter. However, the pirate was too drunk to wage a serious fight and the snake hunter lopped his head off. The snake hunter clawed up jewels and gold and took the horde to his boat. Then he rowed away, leaving behind the dead pirate and his horse.

Many believe that LeBlanc and his Palomino are still on Seahorse Key. Witnesses have reported seeing a headless man riding a long-legged Palomino in the deep of the night on their eternal rounds of the island.

PRINCESS WEENONAH

Silver Springs is located in Marion County about five miles northeast of Ocala. The river that runs through this region has its origin in a deep circular spring, which is about two hundred feet in diameter. A location of breathtaking natural beauty, it is the former home of various Native American peoples.

In the days before the White Man arrived, Okahumkee was the chief of one of these native groups. He was an elderly man, but he had a young beautiful daughter with enchanting black hair named Weenonah. She was an attractive graceful young woman who was the idol of the men. Her father, however, had arranged for her to marry the chief of another group that was friendly to his—even though Weenonah had already fallen in love with another, a man named Chuleotah.

Chuleotah was the young proud chief of a clan that had been engaged in a long feud with Weenonah's people and her father was enraged when he heard of the romance. He declared outright war on Chuleotah and his clan. During the ensuing hostilities, Chuleotah was killed, and as fate had dictated, it was Weenonah's father who delivered the death blow.

The young woman was distraught. She would not return to her father's camp, but instead went to the Silver Spring fountain where she and Chuleotah had often secretly met. There, gazing into the deep crystal water, she beheld the spirit of her slain lover peering longingly up at her. Overcome by her desire to be reunited with him, the young maiden dove into the pool, plunging thirty feet down onto the jagged bed of rocks. She was killed instantly.

Now there are two Native American spirits beneath the waters of the Silver Spring. They inhabit a tranquil world and many people have seen their shadowy forms beneath the water. The long black strands of Weenonah's hair are most frequently observed, streaming forever in the current of time.

TAMPA--
ST. PETERSBURG--
SARASOTA
AREA

RETURN OF THE PROJECTIONIST

The shade of Foster 'Fink' Finley is one of the most well-accepted ghosts I have ever come across. His appearance at the theatre where he had worked for over thirty years is such a common occurrence that he might just as well be one of the current staff.

'Fink' Finley haunts the Tampa Theatre that is in downtown Tampa and is, of course, open to the public. The theatre is a grand showplace designed in 1925 by the famed architect John Amberson. In order to capture the feeling of being outdoors, Mr. Amberson planned the interior of the building with a sweeping openness so that the seats gradually slope down toward the stage and screen rather than doing so on a sharp angle like most theatres.

Outside of the Tampa Theatre. (*Author's photo*)

The ceiling of the Tampa Theatre is a marvel. It is painted dark blue to represent the sky and in Mr. Amberson's day a cloud machine was incorporated in the setting to bedeck the sky with patches of fleecy whiteness behind which twinkling lights shone to give the added effect of stars. It is not hard to understand why Foster Finley never wanted to leave this wonderland!

Finley started working in the Tampa Theatre as a projectionist in the mid-1930s and remained there until his death in 1965. During his earthly life, 'Fink' practically lived at the Tampa Theatre. He would arrive at the building long before its twelve noon opening time and bring with him his shaving equipment and changes of clothes. He often slept overnight in the projection room and never really wanted to leave.

In life, Mr. Finley was a short quiet introverted balding man with beady eyes that were hard to find behind his heavy glasses. He was often seen with a cigarette dangling from the corner of his mouth and was generally described by co-workers as a 'nice guy.' But he was a heavy smoker and was eventually diagnosed with cancer. Even so, he continued to arrive at work and stayed at his post in the projectionist room until the day he collapsed and had to be taken home. 'Fink' Finley never again returned as a mortal to the place he had loved so well.

His ghost, however, returns to the theatre just as diligently as in his former life. His sightings are so numerous as to be overwhelming. Several projectionists have quit because of his presence in the projection booth, although he is not a scary or harmful ghost. In fact, on one occasion he is credited with having found the lost pocket knife of one of the employees who had searched the theatre for it in vain. One day the employee found the knife leaning against the wall in a location it could not have been without his having seen it during his search.

One of the commonest manifestations of the ghost of Foster Finley is the sound of the mass of keys clanging on his key chain. Most employees have heard the clinking of the keys and some have even

The dark interior of the Tampa Theatre where 'Fink' Finley
still roams. (*Author's photo*)

watched doors being unlocked before their eyes by these invisible
keys.

'Fink' Finley still does not want to leave his old and new haunt
and this would probably be one of the few cases where an exorcism
would be of little use. Exorcisms of ghosts are successful generally
because they succeed in informing the departed spirit that he has
died and that it is time for him to move on to another plane. While
the spirit of Mr. Finely may not be completely aware that death has
occurred, it does not seem very likely that he wishes to go to another
plane since he still feels so at home in this one. A séance might be
very interesting if only to get 'Fink's' opinion on the quality of modern movies versus the classic ones he was used to showing.

As noted earlier, the Tampa Theatre is still operating in the heart
of Tampa as of this writing and you can go there and attend movies.
If you do, you may see more than just the movie that is showing on
the screen. Patrons have also witnessed the ghost of 'Fink' Finley

as it floats before the movie screen. He has also been seen leaving the projection room.

If you should attend a movie at the Tampa Theatre and the film suddenly stops rolling, I suggest you look back toward the projection room. You may see the ghost of Foster Finley or you may see the current projectionist fleeing the booth after he has seen Mr. Finley— or you may witness both sights. For an old building built before 1925, there is still a lot of life left in the Tampa Theatre.

THE SPURNED ACTRESS

Another ghost related to the theatre can be found at the University of Tampa. Her name is—or used to be—Bessie Snavely and she can still occasionally be seen at the Falk Theatre located on Kennedy Boulevard. The Kennedy Theatre has been in use since the early days of the twentieth century and has undergone a great deal of restoration since its original opening. It is now a landmark historical building, although performances are still given there. If you ever have the opportunity to take in one of the shows by all means do so—you will not only enjoy a pleasant evening's entertainment but you may also experience a performance by a player from the spirit world.

In the 1930s, both Bessie Snavely and her husband were members of a touring theatre company which put on performances at the Falk Theatre. But Bessie's husband was more interested in another female member of the troupe that he was in her. It was hard to keep this secret from Bessie so, out of hopeless despair, one night she hung herself in one of the locations to which her ghost returns.

Theatre people who perform here, as well as technical crews and patrons, have witnessed other manifestations. The face of a female ghost assumed to be Bessie's has been seen by many people peering sadly down from the lighting booth. Many reports have come from backstage about a sudden flurry of opening and closing of dressing room doors as if by some unseen someone in the act of frantically searching for something or someone.

Loud and rapid pounding has been heard coming from the dressing room where Bessie hung herself. But it has been reported that she can also be a helpful spirit. Sometimes the work of a stage technician can be dangerous such as when he has to work high aloft to make repairs to the lighting system, adjust scenery displays, untangle caught up curtains, adjust the sound system, or do any number of physical tasks that are part of making sure the upcoming performance can be presented to the public as planned.

Many times members of the technical staff have reported being prevented from engaging in an unsafe procedure by a cold hand touching them. It is as if Bessie is standing on guard at the old theatre, protecting those who work and perform there. As noted, her spirit has been seen and felt at many locations throughout the theatre, a place where she seems to feel at home. However, her tragic death at her own hands is the bitter memory that lingers strongest as can be attested to by a visit to her former dressing room, which remains icy cold even during the hottest of Florida afternoons.

GHOST TRESTLE

A trestle, of course, is just a fancy word for a bridge that has train tracks on it. The trestle that we are concerned with is in Brandon, which is on Highway 60 just a few miles east of Tampa. The haunted trestle spans Fish Hawk Creek. It is a difficult hike through wooded and boggy terrain to reach this trestle and it would be wise to get a good knowledge of the area in the daytime before venturing there at night. And you will have to visit the trestle at night if you want to see the apparition which appears around midnight.

At the end of the nineteenth century, a young man named John rode out to this spot on his horse to keep a secret date with his bride-to-be, Martha. At this time, the trestle was still just an ordinary bridge since train tracks had not yet been laid. Something frightened John's horse as it started across the bridge and the steed bolted, throwing its rider down to the river below. John's neck was broken in the fall and he died instantly.

When Martha arrived she found her fiancée's horse wandering aimlessly about the nearby field and she knew something was wrong. The young woman kept her appointment on the bridge but, upon looking over the railing, she saw John's body lying broken on the rocks below. When she examined him and found that her worst fears were true, she lost her mind to grief. She devised a makeshift noose and hung herself from the bridge. Since that time, many people have seen Martha's ghost on the trestle as a radiant green apparition. There have not been any reports of sightings of John.

If you should visit this site, be sure you go to the correct trestle. There is another one not too far away, but it is a much shorter and smaller one. You will be safe if you just remember to look for the ghost on the big trestle and be sure to do your observing around midnight.

THE PROM QUEEN'S GHOST

Prom night. Who hasn't enjoyed the festivities of prom night? Even if a person has never attended a prom, he is aware of what it signifies: glowing high school girls in flowing gowns, eager high school boys in rented tuxedos, and a night of fantasy and revelry. Unfortunately, sometimes it can also turn into a night of tragedy.

The prom queen, Virginia Furry, was looking forward to the night like the other girls. She enjoyed the dancing and food like the other girls. However, unlike many of the other girls, she was willing to live a little riskier this special evening. This included sharing some alcoholic beverages with her date, Paul Erickson. Whether or not this led to the unfortunate incident that occurred later that night of May 1, 1982 was never officially determined.

After the prom, Virginia and Paul—both eighteen—decided to take a drive on a short dark stretch of road which is known as Alternate Keene Road in Largo, Florida. They also had a couple of friends with them. Somehow, Paul lost control of the 1972 Pontiac he was driving and it rammed into a tree, killing him and Virginia. The two teenage passengers who were with them were also injured but they recovered.

Five years later, an odd apparition began appearing along the half mile tract of road where the accident took place. A female ghost in a prom gown will begin to run after a vehicle when it douses its lights upon entering Alternate Keene Road, the local lover's lane. This became such a well-known occurrence that teenagers from the area began flocking there to see the ghost. They even started bringing sleeping bags and camping equipment. Complaints made to the local police put an end to this activity. But the ghost and her tragic story remain, telling of a prom night so long ago that turned bad.

LOST SOUL'S HAVEN

Egmont Key is an island about five miles in circumference and approximately seven miles west of Tampa. A brick lighthouse was built there in 1848, but was leveled by a hurricane. The Key remained dark until 1858 when another lighthouse was built, rising eighty-five feet above sea level.

During the War Between the States, the Union army took over Egmont Key and used it as a prison for captured Confederate soldiers and a safety area for runaway slaves. Three hundred troops were stationed there during the Spanish-American War, but there was no fighting on the Key itself. Except for these war years, Egmont Key was a lonely deserted spot inhabited only by the lighthouse keeper and his family. Of course, that is if you discount the spirits who roam there.

In the last decades of the 1800s, the lighthouse keeper on Egmont Key was Captain Coons and his unusual family. They were all prac-

Egmont Key Lighthouse to which the ghosts of many sailors are attracted. (*Author's photo*)

ticing Spiritualists who found the natural silence and seclusion of the island a perfect place for holding séances. Not surprisingly, the most common visitors to their circle were the souls of deceased sailors. Spirits of people who had drowned in the ocean apparently came to Egmont Key as a haven.

The lighthouse still stands on Egmont Key and flashes its beam toward the Bay. Captain Coons and his family are gone, of course, at least physically. They have probably joined the ranks of spirits who still seek the peaceful haven of Egmont Key.

GHOSTS NEAR THE BAY

Returning to Tampa, we will examine several spirit sightings that have occurred near and in Tampa Bay itself. Our first specter is that of Silas Leland Biglow. He moved to Tampa from Brooklyn, New York, in 1884 and became one of the founding city council members. Being a wealthy entrepreneur, he had a great mansion built in 1908 at Bayshore and Gandy Boulevards. The house was of such grand size that after Silas' death in 1917, it has been used as an artist's studio, a hospital, and a catering hall. Its most recent use has been as an office building.

Even though Silas is dead, he has not left the mansion forever—his ghost frequently returns. Over the years, witnesses have reported seeing his patriarchal spirit striding down the halls of the great building. Other unidentified ghosts have been spotted here as well. The sound of a baby's crying has also been heard by many visitors. It is not surprising that a number of ghosts have been reported at the Biglow Mansion considering all of the uses to which the building has been put and the large number of available witnesses on hand.

Another location where witnesses are not lacking is the Sunshine Skyway Bridge which connects St. Petersburg to the mainland. Until 1980, a mysterious apparition was seen walking along the Skyway Bridge, thumbing a ride. A young blonde female hitchhiker has been spotted here by many people and has been picked up by a few. Those who picked her up were later surprised, however, to find that there was no one in their back seat when they turned to ask their passenger where she wanted to go.

In 1980, the bridge was rammed and severely damaged by the *Summit Venture* as it hauled a cargo of phosphate through the Bay. Since that time there have not been any verified sightings of the young female hitchhiking ghost. Did the ramming accident somehow release the ghost from following her proscribed path on the earthly plane? If so, why? Has something in the balance between realities been jarred out of whack by the crash of the *Summit Venture*? Or has

Sunshine Skyway Bridge frequented by the spirit of a
young woman. (*Author's photo*)

the ghost's path been displaced so that now she is walking out over
the water instead of on the bridge so that no one can see her? No one
knows at this time.

Tampa Bay has been haunted for a very long time by various
apparitions. In the early 1800s, the harbor was guarded by the garrison at Fort Brooke. One day, a fleet of sinister-looking ships was
sighted approaching the shore. Officers were called by the lookouts
and the garrison was called out and readied to meet the invaders.
However, as suddenly as it had appeared on the horizon, the mystery
fleet vanished! The commonly-held explanation is that the ghost
fleet was composed of vessels that had been attacked and sunk by
pirates. But as yet, no one knows for sure the identity of this spectral
fleet.

Not too far awayfrom Tampa Bay is the aptly named 'Ghost
Island. The island is on the west side of the St. Martin's River near

Homosassa. This story of haunting also has its beginnings in the early 1800s when a ship that was heavy with gold was caught up in a hurricane in the waters off the coast of Florida. Members of the crew abandoned their ship, taking with them as much of the treasure as they could. They found refuge on what would later be known as 'Ghost Island' where they promptly began to fight with one another over the gold. During the squabbling, the captain slashed off the first mate's head with a machete. It is the spirit of the headless mate which still roams this gloomy island today.

THE WEEKS HOUSE

Brooksville is a small community about fifty miles north of Tampa and is the site of a haunted house. The Weeks House is located at the corner of Lemon and West Ford Dade Avenues and is abandoned. A driveby or walkby of this location may have ghostly surprises.

The Weeks House looks just like what a haunted house should look like. It is a tall brooding structure that has been vacant for over a decade as of this writing. The wooden floors are warped and decayed, and walls are moldering and crumbling, and atop the rotted roof is the bent weathervane that is precariously close to toppling off the edge. Like many other homes in Florida, the current owners of the Weeks House live up north.

Since the 1970s, this eerie house has changed ownership five times. The ghostly manifestations have played a major role in driving out the occupants and keeping new ones from moving in. Passersby have also witnessed the specters who inhabit this dilapidated old building. Most frequently seen is the figure of a woman standing before one of the front windows. Other curious forms have been seen flitting about before other windows of the gloomy house. Ghastly sounds have also been heard coming from inside the building.

Who these ghosts are and why they are haunting the Weeks House is not known. Judging by the descriptions of the phantoms, a couple of them could belong to the original owners of the house—Jim and Ava Weeks. Could it be that they are sad and angry at the rundown condition into which the house has fallen and have come back to try to do something about it? At one time, it was a warm well-tended house that was home to a loving family. That is how the grand-daughter of Jim and Ava Weeks, Lin, remembers the house.

Perhaps some tragic event occurred in the past in this house which no one knows about. The haunting of the Weeks House remains a mystery. But if there are ghosts there they must be there for a reason. According to Howard Weeks, the son of Jim and Ava Weeks, the spirits in the old house are only imaginary. It might be difficult to convince any of the witnesses of this after they have heard and seen the specters themselves. Especially those five families who have moved out of the haunted building in quick succession.

HAUNTED TOYS

Situated in the town of Brooksville at the corner of May Avenue and Jefferson Street is a renovated nineteenth-century mansion that is now under the care of the Hernando County Historical Society. It is known as the Stringer Mansion and it seems that several of its former occupants are still on the premises.

The house was built in the mid-1850s by John May. After he died, his widow, Marena, married Frank Saxon. But continued misfortune plagued Marena as she saw two of her young children die and then she herself ultimately lost her life in childbirth.

Back then, when laws were not so restrictive, it was not uncommon to bury those in the family who had died in plots on their own property and this is what Mr. Saxon did—his children and his wife are buried in the front yard. This may be the reason why their spirits have remained attached to the great house. Most of the hauntings are attributed to one of the young girls, Jessie May, who died in 1872, three years after the death of her mother. In fact, it was while giving birth to Jessie May that Marena died. Jessie May's sad cries of "Mama! Mama!" for her deceased mother can still be heard echoing through the hallways of the mansion.

Not only is Jessie May's voice often heard, but her apparition is frequently seen frantically wandering through the twelve-room house in a desperate search for her lost mother. She has been seen by many people who have come to tour the renovated mansion and were startled by their encounter with the ghostly girl. The witnesses at first usually believe that Jessie May is simply one of the staff dressed in period clothing. They only learn the truth when they ask the other caretakers about her.

Even though she has been dead for over a century, Jessie May continues to play with the dolls she had loved so much when an occupant of the mortal plane. Caretakers of the museum note that the dolls and other toys that had belonged to little Jessie May are frequently found displaced throughout the house, having been moved from where the staff set them. There are often telltale signs that Jessie May has been playing with her dolls, which are most commonly set upon tiny rocking chairs. Time and again the rocking chairs have been seen moving back and forth on their own accord as if an unseen hand was pushing them. What better comfort is there for a ghostly girl who had lost her mother than to play with the dolls she had loved so well?

It is suspected that other spirits inhabit this four-story house as well. Lights have been seen to go on and off by themselves and the sounds of adult footsteps have been heard in the halls. Is it any wonder that spirits still linger here, considering all the tragic deaths that have occurred in the Stringer Mansion?

THE DON CₑSAR HOTEL

This is one of the most romantic ghost stories I have ever come across. It begins in the 1890s and concerns the star-crossed lovers, Thomas Rowe, and the beautiful black-haired, Lucinda. He was an

The looming Don CeSar Hotel. (*Author's photo*)

American student living abroad in England and she was a budding Spanish opera singer. They met and fell in love while in London and chose to call each other by the names of the two lovers in the opera that Lucinda was singing in—he was Don CeSar and she was Maritana.

Lucinda's parents did not approve of the match, fearing that it would take Lucinda away from her promising opera career. In addition to this, their daughter and Thomas were of different religious faiths. For a time, Thomas and Lucinda engaged in secret rendezvous by a great fountain in London. Here they would talk of the future and how one day Thomas would build a grand hotel by the sea for his love.

Eventually, however, Lucinda's parents were successful in destroying the romance and Thomas returned home to America brokenhearted. Then, two years after their parting, Thomas learned of Lucinda's death and received a deathbed letter from her in which she wrote, "Time is infinite. I wait for you by our fountain . . . to share our timeless love . . . forever, Maritana."

Thomas moved to St. Petersburg in the 1920s and there he built the grand hotel he had long dreamed of, naming it the Don CeSar. It was a magnificent tribute to his lost love and was designed in the Moorish style with a vast courtyard bedecked with a glorious fountain. Thomas lived on the premises and was very much involved in the day-to-day activities of the hotel, often meeting with the guests and making sure they were happy with the accommodations.

Thomas Rowe died in 1940. Soon after his death, the hotel was sold to the military and was turned into a Veterans' Administration hospital in 1945. Numerous renovations took place after this, resulting in the closing of the vast lobby and the destruction of the fountain. Finally, in 1973, a serious effort to restore the great structure was made and the Don CeSar became an operating resort hotel once more.

It was with the renovations in the 1970s that the ghost of Thomas Rowe made his first appearance. He has been sighted in many locations throughout the hotel, including the dining room and the lobby and elevator—only to disappear into the crowd. He has frequently been seen talking to the guests and asking them if their dinners were to their liking and if the accommodations were satisfactory, just as he used to do in life.

But, unlike during his life, Thomas Rowe has been reunited with his lost love, Lucinda, at their dream castle by the sea. He and a young woman attired in theatrical costume, have been seen on many occasions, strolling hand-in-hand along the beach as well as through the lobby of the hotel.

Thomas Rowe's ghost is a very active one and is always concerned about the safety and well-being of his modern day guests. In 1990, photographic teams from two magazines—*Southern Bride* and the *Condé Nast Traveler*—came to the Don CeSar to use the beautiful setting as backdrops for shooting layouts. An editor on the staff of *Southern Bride* was approached by Thomas' ghost in her suite one day and was advised not to take a picture in the planned shooting location the next day. The specter then disappeared. The editor ig-

Above: Lobby of the Don CeSar Hotel where the original owner has been seen greeting guests. (Author's photo)

The Don CeSar's main dining room where the original owner's ghost has often appeared. (*Author's photo*)

nored the ghost's warning and attempted to take the photographs any-way—only to find out that her crew's efforts were time and again thwarted by a particularly persistent black crow. Since the photo-graphic team was forced to abandon that location, it was never known what the reason for the warning was all about.

Sightings of Thomas Rowe and Lucinda continue until the present time, even though the management doesn't officially encourage re-ports of them. It would be hard to find a more dedicated caretaker for this grand hotel than the man who built it and was so interested in the comfort and safety of its guests. He has even re-turned from the afterlife to carry on these functions. More than that, he has brought a friend with him—his beloved Lucinda. If you ever have a chance to stay at the Don CeSar Hotel and meet a well-dressed middle-aged man who inquires about your satisfaction with the ac-commodations, do not forget to ask his name—it might just be Tho-mas Rowe.

HAUNTED ST. PETERSBURG HIGH

St. Petersburg is located directly southwest of Tampa across Tampa Bay. While it is common to refer to Tampa and St. Petersburg in one breath as if they are somehow joined together, this is not true. They are two distinct cities separated by quite a bit of water.

St. Petersburg is a large city which has a great many schools. One of its former schools is a haunted place. Called 'Old St. Petersburg High,' the building has been converted into condominiums, but whether or not the ghost has been converted into a spirit who has gone on to the next plane of existence is another matter.

When the structure was still a high school, it was the Bell Build-ing and held the administrative offices for the school. One of the ghost's favorite offices to haunt was the dean's office. Maybe it was because it was where the ghost's favorite chair was located. Or per-haps it was because the spirit belongs to a recalcitrant former pupil who had spent a lot of time in the dean's office and was now trying to get back at the head of the school in the afterlife.

At any rate, this ghost has frequently been caught in the dean's office rocking in an empty chair. The spirit has not been seen in the chair; it is the rocking that has been witnessed by members of the startled staff and the dean.

Disturbances have also occurred in one of the rooms where the teachers gathered to go over and organize their paperwork. An unseen force performed ghostly antics that included the tossing of test papers up to the ceiling. This seems to be more evidence pointing toward the ghost belonging to a former disgruntled student. What better way to take revenge on a teacher than to throw his or her carefully-collated paperwork into the air?

The only time that a sighting is made it is always just a fleeting glimpse. Staff have reported on several occasions being shocked by an unrecognizable featureless face peering around a hallway corner that disappears before anyone can track down the tricky specter. Once again it seems that we are observing the actions of a prank-playing unruly high school student. Another characteristic of this ghost is the scent of perfume that precedes its manifestation. Does this then suggest that the high-spirited ghost was a female student in its former life?

As of yet, no definite identity has been put forward as to who this ghost is. Maybe the people who are running the association that is overseeing the condominiums that the ghost is now haunting will have better luck at finding out who did it. Perhaps they could call upon her to fill in when they are one short for bridge or shuffleboard.

A POLTERGEIST IN SARASOTA

Sarasota is the winter home for a great many people who spend the rest of their time up north—they are called 'snowbirds' by the local residents. Located on the Gulf Coast about fifty miles south of

Tampa, Sarasota is a renowned artist's haven and boasts many multi-million dollar mansions. It is generally a peaceful city whose population is about fifty thousand people during the off season. When Hallowe'en nears, the snowbirds being winging their way down until there is a huge flock of them here by New Years.

Sarasota is the home of at least one playful poltergeist who likes to annoy the former clerk of Sarasota at his new home. The sound of footsteps shuffling down the hallway outside the McLelland family bedrooms in the middle of the night is a common occurrence. Since they are never sure if it is a flesh-and-blood intruder, someone from the family always has to check out the noise. So far only a disembodied spirit has been found pacing the hallways. Having an unseen house guest like the McLelland's can be a nuisance at times. Pictures have been seen flying off the walls and various other household items have been transported to spots where they should not be.

One night about two in the morning, the mischievous spirit played a particularly imaginative prank. It woke up the entire household by an incessant ringing of the doorbell. The family dog growled and barked and Mr. McLelland grumbled all the way on his journey to the front door. It was not until he got to the door that he realized that their house did not have a doorbell!

Although the McLellands have attempted to research the origin of their ghostly visitor they have not had much luck. At least their poltergeist is of the playful variety—it certainly does a good imitation of a doorbell!

THE TROUBLED SANDLIN HOUSE

The Sandlin House was built in 1893 by James and Mary Sandlin and today stands as a public landmark on West Retta Esplanade in Punta Gorda. It is a magnificent Victorian home designed in the Southern plantation-style. It is a picturesque sight as it gazes out

The Sandlin House in Punta Gorda which is haunted by the spirit
of fourteen-year-old Mary Leah Sandlin. (*Author's photo*)

across a park and a wide bay. Punta Gorda, meaning 'Fat Point,' is
located on the west coast of Florida and is easily reached by I-75. To
get to the Sandlin House, exit on Highway 17, head west, and follow
the signs to Gilchrest Park, which fronts West Retta Esplanade. There
are a number of vintage homes on this street and the Sandlin House
is one of the most impressive.

Like many family homes built during the early days of Florida's
past, the Sandlin House is graced with lore and history. It was built
by one of the early powerful families as were so many of the grand
estates we will be visiting. James Sandlin amassed a fortune in real
estate as well as by raising and selling cattle and various other inter-
ests. Sandlin bought a good portion of the land that would become
the outskirts of the city of Punta Gorda when it was still overgrown
terrain on the edge of the Peace River.

In 1886, Mr. Sandlin also bought the heart of the tiny town of
Trabue, which in a few years would become the heart of Punta Gorda.
Next the railroad came to Punta Gorda followed by the speculators

and then the masses. James Sandlin now owned the choicest real estate in town.

Mr. Sandlin took part in two first-ever events in the history of Punta Gorda. His marriage to Mary Leah Sandlin was the first on record and the birth of their son a year later was the first birth registered there. Unfortunately, the Sandlin's first born died three days later without having been named. This was to be the first of many sad events to befall this well-known and important family.

Several children were born to the Sandlins: Felix Knowles, James Henry, Mary Leah, Bessie, and Reid Ware. Felix died in 1902 at the age of eleven from unknown causes and Mary was killed in a tragic accident in 1909. The Sandlins came to know that neither their wealth nor power could protect them from the misfortunes that befall all people.

James Sandlin contracted tuberculosis, which was very common at the time, and moved with his family to their other home in Alligator Creek, hoping that his health would improve. It didn't and he died in 1903. James Sandlin was buried next to his son, Felix, at Indian Springs Cemetery. This cemetery is an atmospheric graveyard set back in the rustic wooded countryside and can be reached by taking Exit 27 west and following the signs. Many of the area's historic figures are buried here and it is well worth the visit. You might even spot an elusive ghost or two.

After James Sandlin died, his wife moved back to their estate on West Retta Esplanade with her three remaining children. Tragedy was to strike again and this time involved one of the most mundane day-to-day activities. Fourteen-year-old Mary Leah had taken the laundry out to the front porch to do the ironing. She was using a newly-purchased gasoline-heated iron that had been touted as the modern labor-saving device. Somehow gasoline escaped from the iron, formed a pool at Mary's feet, and ignited. Using both her long dress and the nearby laundry as additional fuel, the fire quickly engulfed the girl. Mary was rushed to the hospital, but died a few hours later. The spot where she had been standing on the porch had been deeply scorched and still cannot be properly painted over.

The porch where Mary Leah Sandlin tragically died in
an ironing accident. (*Author's photo*)

In 1925, Mrs. Sandlin sold the house to Frank Smoak, Senior. It
is from this time that the first ghostly occurrences originated. Mr.
Smoak reported that on many occasions he heard the front door open
and the sound of footsteps crossing the entrance hall and then climbing the stairs. The footsteps always lead to what used to be the bedroom of Mary Leah.

In the 1960s, the Sandlin House came under the ownership of
Julie Hollander. She, too, reported ghostly occurrences that also
pointed to Mary Leah as the initiator. The iron Ms. Hollander used
for pressing clothes would mysteriously turn itself on and off and she
would often find laundry that she had just neatly folded to have been
taken from the basket and hurled around the room. Taking into account Mary Leah's sad end, her hostility toward ironing equipment
and laundry is understandable. Even ghosts display tempers. At
least Mary does seem to have found some peace in being able to
return to the quiet of her old bedroom, a place that was probably a
refuge to her in life as well as now in death.

HAUNTED CAYO PELAU ISLE

Hundreds of tiny isles are strong along the coastline of Florida. Many of them are well-hidden and in days long past provided excellent retreats for pirates and privateers. Lost treasures are still buried on these secluded islands, as are members of crew of pirate ships and their wives. Ghostly tales are associated with many of these sites and one, Cayo Pelau, is also cursed.

Cayo Pelau is located just inside of the northern border of Lee County. To reach Cayo Pelau, take Exit 32 (Toledo Blade) off I-75 and travel toward Port Charlotte. Continue on this road until you reach Highway 776 and follow it toward El Jobean. Follow this road for about ten miles and then turn left on the road toward Placida on Route 771. Finally, head straight until you reach Gasparilla Island and the town of Boca Grand. Directly east of Gasparilla Island is Cayo Palau. Now your difficulties begin. You can only get to Cayo Pelau by boat and it is not easy getting someone to ferry you there. Remember, this island is both haunted and cursed and bad things happen to people who visit there. It is just the type of scenario you read about in fictional ghost stories or have seen on television or at the movies. But here it's real!

Cayo Pelau is deserted right now. Hopefully development will not reach this far and destroy the natural hauntedness of the site. Development is another major curse in Florida as precious real estate is ruined without anyone seeming to realize they are not only stripping away the character of the state, but also wrecking the environment that makes it so beautiful and unique.

Cayo Pelau is overgrown with palm and palmetto and its forest paths are darkened with the thick ghostly webbing of Spanish moss. It is quiet here except for the sounds of birds, insects, and the skitterings of the armadillos rooting through the underbrush. Then there are the ghostly wails and voices that come drifting from the depths of the forest.

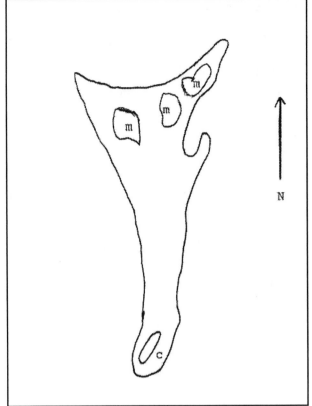

Drawing of Cayo Pelau Islan showing locations of native American burial mounds (m) and the early nineteenth century cemetery (C).

Legend has it that the ghostly apparitions belong to pirates and the women they had taken as wives who had died there. The pirate that made Florida famous, Jose Gaspar, was said to have used Cayo Pelau as a retreat from his swashbuckling and came here to drink, carouse and . . . read. His main home was supposed to be on Gasparilla Island just across the bay—a very romantic story and a perfect explanation for supernatural activity. The only problem is that Jose Gaspar was a myth.

Most people in Florida will recognize the name of Jose Gaspar (or Gasparilla) and tell you he was a famous pirate—although they do not realize that he was wholly invented by a man named Juan Gomez. Gomez was a fishing guide in the late 1800s who concocted wild tales to bolster his business. The swashbuckling adventures of Jose Gaspar is one of his more remarkable fables. The 'infamous pirate' is even celebrated with a festival in Tampa once a year when the city is besieged by men in pirate costume. It is a lot of fun and a good attraction—but not based on fact.

The inventor of Gaspar also claimed to be a former cabin boy to the pirate. In reality, Gomez was born in Nicaragua and was seventy-three years old when died (in 1900) by drowning after being tangled in his own fishing net at Panther Key.

In 1819 the United States acquired Florida from Spain at any of his legendary crew, who do they belong to? For an island that today is abandoned there are many candidates. Excavations at Cayo Pelau reveal that the tiny island may have been the site of a Spanish-speaking people as early as 1670. However, Indian burial mounds at the northern end of the island testify to even earlier inhabitants.

In 1819, the United States acquired the Florida from Spain at which time four Spanish citizens filed claims to the portions of the island where they lived. Their claims were denied. In 1896, most of the southern part of the island was sold to the Florida Southern Railway. At this time, there were roughly seventy people living on Cayo Pelau.

For an unknown reason, Cayo Pelau was abandoned and by 1900 had become an island of ghost towns. The last person to live on the island was Columbus McLeod, an Audubon warden, who was stationed there to put a stop to illegal plume hunting to supply feathers for ladies' hats. Mr. McLeod was murdered under mysterious circumstances on November 30, 1908. His boat was found sunk in the bay, weighted down by two heavy sacks of sand. The warden's hat was discovered with two large gashes in it, probably made by an ax, and in the cuts were found hair and a large amount of blood. McLeod's body was never found and probably had been devoured by alligators or sharks.

Yes, there are many candidates for who might be spooking Cayo Pelau, chief among them Mr. McLeod. However, judging by the amount of activity there as well as how widely it is distributed and by the variety of the apparitions it seems highly likely that there are many spirits trapped on this tiny island. Fleeting ghostly figures have been reported all across the island as well as bobbing ghost lights and the sounds of moaning and wailing.

Add this to the well-known and often experienced curse that befalls visitors to Cayo Pelau and you can understand why it is so difficult to get transportation there. A number of cases have been reported about boat engines that had run perfectly well before coming to this island suddenly acting up in these cursed waters, sputtering and dying only to be started again with great difficulty. Numerous are the treasure hunters who'd braved the trip here with metal detectors in hand only to find that their coin-locating devices suddenly didn't function properly anymore on this cursed soil.

The vapor of the past hangs thickly over Cayo Pelau. Whether it is cast by the ancient Indian mound builders, the Spanish settlers, the privateers, the brutally-murdered Audubon warden, or by all of their combined spirits it is a definite warning they are sending to all intruders. Visitors come at your own risk!

THE SACRED ORE

This is a heart-warming ghost story. At its center is a loving Swedish grandmother who returns from the grave to check on the health of her family still on this earth.

This true story begins in 1837 with the arrival of the Johansen family at Sanford, Florida, as part of the first wave of emigrants from Sweden. There were six people in the Johansen family, including the parents, Grandma Johansen, and three children, Isabelle, Edna, and Ruth. Soon after arriving in America the family moved to Arcadia, Florida where Papa Carl purchased a sawmill. Because of Papa Carl's bad asthma, however, the Johansen's sold the sawmill and moved to Lemon Bay in Englewood to be near the salt air.

At this new place, Carl Johansen purchased another sawmill and on September 14, 1907, he bought a stretch of land on the beach from the well-known hermit of Palm Ridge—Giles W. Chapman. This is where Carl built his home, the Hermitage—not to be confused with the famous museum of St. Petersburg, Russia or the slightly less famous one in St. Petersburg, Florida.

The old one-story wooden building still survives and under the auspices of the Sarasota County Commission it was preserved and moved back a few hundred feet from the rapidly-eroding shoreline. It is one of the oldest buildings on Manasota Key and ironically enough, it was moved to the site of a mass grave whose occupants met with foul play on a large scale. That mystery remains unsolved.

The Hermitage in 1992. It is haunted by the ghost of Grandma Johansen. (*Author's photo*)

To reach Manasota Key, follow the same directions for Cayo Pelau with the exception that you do not leave Route 776 but follow it directly into Englewood. From here follow the signs toward Manasota Key where you will find the haunted remains of the Hermitage.

After finally settling for good in their Hermitage home in Englewood, the Johansen's lived the old-fashioned life of hard work and close family activities particular to life in the early 1900s. Carl worked hard and long at his sawmill, rowing himself there every day across the bay because back then there was no bridge connecting the key with the mainland.

Also at that time, Manasota Key was thick with pine trees that provided the wood for the mill. The trees were hewn down, sawed in the mill, and then rafted across Lemon Bay. It was not all hard work because sometimes Carl's daughter joined him during the rafting of the sawed lumber and would catch mullet and pompano and various other fish as they leapt into the air and fell at their feet. The 'catch' would end up in Grandma Johansen's kitchen where they were prepared into a fine meal. She did all of the baking for the family even though Carl's wife, Anna, had once been head cook for the King of Sweden!

Grandma Johansen prepared much more than food in her specially-designed kitchen. She had her own home apothecary from which she brewed various remedies for many of the assorted ailments that commonly besets families. When an illness proved to be uncommonly stubborn and didn't respond to her homemade medicines she resorted to burning a lump of sacred lead over which she intoned prayers from her Swedish Bible. The person who had been taken ill was invariably cured by this method of doctoring. Grandma Johansen kept her precious chunk of lead hidden in an old clock that hung above the table in her room. Only her daughter, Anna, knew where it was hidden.

But Grandma Johansen was well up in age when the move to America was made and now she herself contracted a serious ailment. Day-by-day her condition worsened but she would not burn the sacred lead for her own recovery. Finally, she was taken back to the family's more comfortable house in Arcadia where she could spend her last days in more pleasant surroundings. Then, worn out from age and illness, Grandma Johansen died.

After her death, the Johansen's moved back to the Hermitage in Englewood. That is when the ghostly phenomenon began to occur.

Manasota Key, site of the Hermitage. (*Author's photo*)

In the quiet of the night, the sound of Grandma's window rising was heard followed by a sudden slam as it banged closed again. Upon investigation all the windows were found to be tightly closed and still barred.

Anna Johansen thought she understood what the matter might be. Something in Grandma Johansen's room was disturbing the dead woman's spirit, keeping her from achieving peace. Anna remembered the scared lead that was hidden in the old clock in her room. She removed the chunk of metal, took it out behind the house, dug a hole in the sand, and buried it. Anna concluded the ritual with some prayers and by giving a brief message to her deceased mother describing how she had buried the sacred lead.

This ended the ghostly noises at the Hermitage . . . for a while. A few years later when the children, now grown, returned to the Hermitage, they reported still hearing ghostly noises from Grandma's room. One of them is a well-known Englewood historian who recalls hearing spooky noises arising from the house when he was camping out with some friends as a youngster. At that time, he was not aware that the house was reputed to be haunted.

The last resident of the house lived there for eleven years without experiencing any problems. Before moving out, she invited a local psychic to stay in the Hermitage and sleep in Grandma Johansen's old bed. The psychic accepted the offer, but fled from the haunted room after the first night. She said that the ghostly presence in the room made it too uncomfortable for her to sleep there.

It is apparent then, that the sprit of Grand Johansen has not yet left this earthly plane and in fact is still very much inhabiting her old bedroom. Perhaps it is the wholesome quality of life that she had led in the Hermitage that keeps her bound to the old house and the old ways. Maybe she is coming back again and again to tend to the health of the family she had loved so dearly. Or could it be that she would have preferred to die here instead of in the house in Arcadia to which she had been moved when she was ill?

One thing that seems certain is that Grandma Johansen's haunting of the old house is not a malevolent type of manifestation. Her granddaughters revealed that there were never any hauntings when they were children and they only began when they were older, as if their grandmother purposefully did not want to scare them.

How to account for the actions of a ghost? Sometimes ghosts seem to return simply because they want to.

THE HIDDEN CEMETERY

Until not too long ago, segregation was the rule in the South—a rule that extended even to the ultimate division of death. Even cemeteries were segregated. Often the existence of the usually poorly-located and poorly-maintained cemetery set aside for 'colored' people was forgotten after it was no longer used and it eventually became part of the landscape.

Such was the case of the 'colored cemetery' at Harbor View in the county of Port Charlotte. In the middle of the nineteenth century, this was the burial ground of 'coloreds' in the Charlotte Harbor area who, until 1986, had laid in peace, undisturbed, and at rest. Then the developers moved in. As usual, it was then that the trouble began and the natural landscape and all that lived—or has died—in that environment was thrown into upheaval. But, on rare occasions, such as we see in this story, those souls who have been so thoughtlessly disturbed successfully fought back.

Florida was the third state to secede from the Union in the War Between the States, preceded by South Carolina and Mississippi, in that order. At the outset of the war, there was a Union fort at Fort Myers, which is roughly thirty miles south of where our story takes place. The fort was manned by Black enlisted men, but was commanded by White officers.

The garrison at Fort Myers is important to our story because the central figures who haunt the forgotten 'colored' cemetery in Charlotte Harbor were at one time stationed there. During the War Between the States, Fort Myers came under Southern control, but once the capitulation at Appomattox was made, the North regained control of the garrison. This saw the return of one of its former officers, Nathan DeCoster, and a number of Black soldiers who had served with him: Joseph Chapman, Richard Hambilton, Mitchell Harrison, and John Lomans.

The years following the War Between the States were in many ways as brutal for the South as the War had been. It was the so-called era of 'Reconstruction,' at which time Blacks were placed in positions of authority all across the South, even though very few of them could read or write. Many Southerners were infuriated by this state of affairs and thus was ushered in the era of the 'Regulators.' Regulators were vigilantes who took the law into their own hands and struck out at the Northern sympathizers and Blacks. Once the federal government withdrew its occupying army from Fort Myers on July 25, 1869, the regulators were free to unleash their terror.

Blacks who had been left in charge by the Northerners were among the first to be attacked. They were ridden down in the street after which they were horsewhipped and shotgunned. They were torn from their offices and beaten and brutalized. They were set upon at home and at their local gathering places. Although not everyone sympathized with the actions of the Regulators, there were few who could stand up to them, even the sheriff and his deputies. The federal government didn't seem to care either.

John Lomans was the target of repeated assaults. He was one of the Blacks who had served with the North during the War at Fort Myers and who had returned to the South after the War with Nathan DeCoster. John Lomans was one of the few Blacks who had received an education and could read and write and was consequently appointed voter registrar. It was while he was engaged in riding across the countryside registering Black voters that he first set upon.

In an officially-prepared affidavit, Mr. Lomans described how he was attacked by three local brothers—Gus, Alonzo, and John Johnson—who dragged him from his horse and mercilessly horse-whipped and beat him. That time they stopped just short of killing him, but a few months later Mr. Lomans was once again beset by a pack of Regulators. This time they were intent on finishing the job and had just placed a noose around his neck when he was saved by a man named William Hollingsworth who had ridden over to see what all the commotion was about.

Despite the dangerous nature of his work, Mr. Lomans bravely stayed on and somehow survived. Many Blacks did not survive. Jim Parnell and William Lewis were shotgunned to death. Nathaniel Redd was lynched. The graves in the segregated 'colored' cemetery continued to increase. Most of the Blacks were scared out of the area. John Lomans was one of the few who remained and who died a natural death. He owned a farm that he worked with his wife, Esther, and their four children: Mary, Francis, George, and Cinderella. Eleven other children had died earlier. John, his wife, and children were all buried in the 'colored' cemetery.

One or all of their spirits are most likely the ones haunting this area. They are the ones who have been disturbed from their just rest by the arrival of the new scourge from the North—developers. The site of the old 'colored' graveyard where they were buried was cleared and became the location for a restaurant on the Tamiami Trail in Charlotte Harbor. The owner wishes the name and address of the restaurant to be kept secret. Perhaps he is trying to keep bad luck from befalling him and his business, which is something several other owners of restaurants at that same location have been unable to fend off. Since the construction of this building on the Tamiami Trail, a string of restaurant businesses there have failed. Is there a curse over this old burial ground?

There are certainly ghosts still lingering there. Towels sail through the air on their own, faucets turn themselves on and off, dishes suddenly leap off the shelves, and mysterious fires flare up for no known reason. The spirits of those buried beneath the foundation of this building seem quite angry and unrelenting. However, they do seem to be getting a measure of revenge—which is more than many ghosts accomplish. And it seems that they intend to keep up their ghostly protesting until they have the solemnity of their burial ground reinstated. This, however, may take quite some time because developers are not known for returning what they have plundered. But the spirit of a man like John Lomans is not one to give up a fight.

MIAMI AREA

SCARING UP A DISCOUNT

Often when a store has a slightly damaged item it is sold at a discount. One warehouse in Miami would have produced a great number of discounted items due to the workings of a very busy poltergeist. The problem began in the middle of December, 1966, at the height of the Christmas shopping season. All of a sudden, objects began flying off the shelves in the Tropication Arts warehouse that specialized in novelty items. What eventually took place here was certainly a novelty, but not much to the liking of part-owner Alvin Laubheim. The high amount of breakage could not be ignored and it seemed that the obvious cause of it were two shipping clerks, Julio Vasquez and Curt Hagemayer. Even though both denied it, boxes continued to fly off the warehouse shelves and items continued to be broken. Mr. Laubheim had kept a close watch on the suspect employees, but much to his surprise he did not see them cause any breakage. Objects flew off the shelves when neither of the two shipping clerks were anywhere near the location of the damage.

Noting that what was occurring seemed like magical tricks, the other part-owner of the warehouse, Glen Lewis, did something quite unusual: he called in a magician friend, Howard Brooks, to investigate. After closely examining the strange phenomenon and attempting to magically duplicate it, Mr. Brooks was nonplused. He did not want to admit that the activity taking place was caused by a ghost, but neither could he explain it.

On January 14, 1967, the police were summoned to look into the latest case of 'vandalism.' Patrolman William Killin arrived on the scene to investigate and he began to question the employees. While he was doing so, four objects fell off the shelves behind him. He was so bewildered by this event that he called for assistance. After more police came and more examinations of the scene were conducted, the verdict was that they had no explanation for what was causing the mysterious breakage. Nevertheless, the investigation continued and it was determined that the disturbances were not the result of

Young man who incited the Miami poltergeist (Archives photo)

sonic booms, the accumulation of underground gas, or water currents. Nor were any of the neighboring businesses afflicted by the same type of unusual activity as at the Tropication Arts warehouse.

Then the ghost hunters and parapsychologists took over. The well-known writer, Suzy Smith, was among them and she took up steady surveillance of the warehouse shipping clerks as they went about their work routine. She saw boxes shift by themselves, float off the shelves and fall to floor—none of them in the vicinity of the workers. A box of rubber daggers dropped in one aisle while a box of china sailfish sailed off a shelf in another aisle.

Next to arrive was the famous poltergeist-chaser William Roll. He immediately developed a series of 'target areas,' which were shelves that he had closely examined to make certain that no trickery could be involved if any objects were disturbed in these locations. The 'target areas' were not free from assault: boxes flung themselves to the floor there as willingly as at any other spot.

The investigation finally centered around the previously mentioned shipping clerk, Julio Vasquez. He was a disgruntled nineteen-year-old who had a strong dislike for this boss, Mr. Laubheim, but could not vent his anger in public for fear of being fired. Since the poltergeist activity only occurred when Julio was around he became a suspect. He was not suspected of physically causing the breakage, but psychically through telekinesis. The evidence against him grew stronger when, while Julio was undergoing testing in a laboratory setting, a vase fell off a shelf by itself and rolled to his feet.

While the poltergeist activity at the Tropication Arts warehouse remains a mystery, it is an odd coincidence that stopped as soon as Julio Vasquez was fired.

A HAUNTED VILLA

It took Cliff Ensor a very long time to sell his haunted villa located in a section of Miami known as Little Haiti. The villa had been on the market for over ten years, despite the historical background of the building. The villa at 5811 N. Miami Avenue was built in 1925. Having once served as the Cuban consulate, this neo-classical building has ten rooms, sixteen-foot ceilings, doors made of mahogany, and exquisite antique furniture. Not only has the physical sense of the past been preserved here, but also the spiritual past in the form of ghosts. One of the spirits that haunts the villa is believed to belong to Paula, the wife of the first consul. She is most often seen in the living room where Paula's grand piano used to be. Not surprisingly, piano music has been heard arising from this room.

While the ghost of Paula has not demonstrated any frightening qualities, the front gate of the villa seems to be possessed of a will of its own. It, however, displays definite violent tendencies. On calm days when there is no wind, the gate has swung closed under its own power, trapping at least three cats in its jaws. All three of the unlucky felines were strangled to death in the gate's clutches.

It is quite ironic, however, that while cats avoid the haunted living room, they do not avoid the deadly gate. Psychics have been known to avoid the haunted living room as well. At least one psychic attempted to remain the night there, but was driven from the haunted room and suffered such horrors that he would not even speak of the experience afterwards.

No one has every truly explained the reasons for the unearthly phenomena that occur in the villa. The building was eventually sold at auction at a much reduced price. The ghosts have apparently decided to remain.

OUTRAGEOUS, ODD, AND ECCENTRIC GHOSTS AROUND THE STATE

OUTRAGEOUS GHOSTS

The following stories are old country tales of some of the most bizarre hauntings I have ever come across. They involve a woman who refused to wear undergarments, a lit-up cemetery, a wandering bride, and a wildman. All four stories have assumed legendary proportions in their respective areas of Florida and each is a true event.

The story of the wife who refused to wear undergarments takes place in Lafayette County. Lafayette is in the northern part of Florida just at the point where the panhandle begins to turn to the west. Approximately half of the country is swampland and the few towns that exist in Lafayette County are set deep in the country.

The woman in question might be accused of having 'loose morals.' She didn't wear undergarments beneath her outerwear, which was tattered to the point of being almost see-through. Her husband didn't like her flimsy attire and was constantly upbraiding her and trying to get her to change her wardrobe to something less revealing. Apparently he suspected that she dressed as she did to be ready for any visitors who might drop by when he was away tending to the fields.

The woman chose to remain in her teasing ensemble and would not even change into more modest clothing when visitors came to the house. This infuriated her husband and he eventually grabbed and ax and cut off his wife's head. After he killed her, he hung himself. Both bodies were found and buried on their own farmland. Sometime later, the house where they had lived mysteriously burned down.

The pump that was beside the house was not destroyed and still remains. It is here that the ghost of the wife appears on moonlit nights, working the pump handle with one hand while keeping her head nestled under her free arm. All the while, she can be heard making the most piteous moaning sounds. Witnesses to this sighting also claim that water comes from the pump as the ghost works the handle. There have not been any reports of the husband's ghost.

The next outrageous haunting occurs in a town called Wassica, another secluded community deep in the countryside. Wassica is in Jefferson County and is located on Highway 59 and about fifty miles east of Tallahassee. Just outside of Wassica is Broomsage Cemetery. The first paranormal events in this graveyard were reported by James Burt Roach in the early part of the twentieth century. At various times in his life—which began on February 7, 1897—Mr. Roach was a miller, a logger, and a farmer.

After dusk one day, Mr. Roach and his son-in-law, Willie Gray, walked out to Broomsage Cemetery for a little peace and quiet after a hard afternoon's work. Unfortunately, they didn't get a very long or peaceful rest. Shortly after seating themselves among the tombstones, a man suddenly appeared in their midst out of nowhere. Then the entire cemetery lit up in a great flash of white light which did not dissipate, but kept the whole area under bright illumination. Terrified, Mr. Roach and Willie leapt to their feet and madly dashed from the scene. The legend of haunted Broomsage Cemetery was born.

Several years later, a second manifestation occurred there. Wilton Boland, a local resident, was at Broomsage Cemetery one day when he beheld the vision of James Roach Story's wife in the graveyard. James Roach Story is one of the kinfolk of the man who had witnessed the first sighting. The wife of James Story had been dead for fifteen years at the time of Wilton Boland's encounter with her in the cemetery. She was walking amidst the gravestones wearing a flowing white gown.

A third paranormal event at Broomsage Cemetery was reported by an outsider, a truck driver, in 1947. William Clark was looking for a shortcut on his route and decided to detour through Broomsage Cemetery. It was night and pitch dark except for the headlights of his truck. Then, all of a sudden, it was bright as day. The entire graveyard was awash in intense white light, just like the first paranormal event fifty years before. Not knowing what to make of this, Mr. Clark sped the rest of the way through the cemetery without stopping until he reached the town where he told his story. His listeners were not surprised.

Traveling south from Jefferson County, our next stop is Venice in the middle of Florida along the west coast. The town is primarily known for the extreme age of its citizenry. It has been said that parents of the other retirees in Florida make their homes in Venice. Naturally, it is a quiet pretty little community with numerous antique and gift shops. Venice is also home to the bride by the water fountain.

The house where this haunting occurs is on Nassau Street and can be identified by the large fountain in the backyard that is adorned with a statue of the god Pan. It is one of the oldest houses in Venice and was purchased by a bridegroom for his bride as a gift. Unfortunately, the bride died on her wedding day. However, this has not prevented her from enjoying her gift house because her spirit has

House on Nassau Street in Venice where the ghost of a young
bride has been seen. (*Author's photo*)

been spotted here on many occasions. She is seen either peering out the windows or taking a stroll in her wedding gown around the fountain in the back. The ghost bride apparently prefers the fountain because it is where she has been sighted most often.

Back yard of the Nassau Street house where the bride's
ghost walks. (*Author's photo*).

The ghost of the 'wildman of Englewood' is sometimes seen
at the end of this street. (*Author's photo*)

Not too far south of Venice is the community of Englewood. In the early part of the twentieth century a genuine wildman made his home here. No one ever knew the man's name, not even the people who operated the insane asylum in Chattahoochee where he had been incarcerated. Before his days in the madhouse, the wildman used to live in the palm hammocks that stood at the location of the present-day St. Raphael's Church in Englewood. He spent most of his time hanging out behind the Lemon Bay Trading Company Store and lived off the scraps that were tossed out back.

The wildman has been dead a good many years, but his ghost returns to its old haunt where the hammock stand used to be. His apparition usually appears at dusk and has been seen at the end of Yale Street silhouetted against the Bay. He presents quite startling sight looming out of the woods, still as wild and unkempt as ever.

THE BRONZE APPARITION

Another one of our Florida eccentrics-turned-ghost is Waldo Sexton. He lived in, and still haunts, Vero Beach on Highway 1 on the east coast of Florida about midway down its length.

Florida is a state that is known for being flat. You will not find too many high places here. Apparently, this was a situation that Waldo Sexton could not abide so he set out to do something about it. One day in the early 1960s, he began construction on what would eventually become known as 'Waldo's Mountain.' Day after day, he hauled load after load of sand and loose dirt onto his property. What started as a small hill became a large mound and then eventually a little dome-shaped mountain.

When Waldo had completed his great work, he carved a long flight of stairs into its side. He was not quite finished yet, however. Waldo climbed the fifty feet or so to the summit of the mountain and planted two chairs on the crest. Once his work was finally finished, he donated it to the City of Vero Beach—his hometown.

Waldo Sexton died in 1967, a short while after his project was completed. Unfortunately, the City of Vero Beach neither appreciated the grandeur of the man-made mountain nor the gesture of its donation. Five years after Waldo died, his marvelous monument to elevation was leveled.

A restaurant was eventually built on the site and that is when the trouble began. Loli Heuser, the owner of the restaurant, suddenly found strange things happening at her establishment. Glasses that she had been holding in her hand shattered of their own accord. On other occasions, objects began flying off the walls. Obviously, Waldo's spirit was not happy with what had become of his hard-built mountain.

One of Loli Heuser's most memorable encounters with Waldo Sexton's ghost happened one night after closing, when the image of the late mountain-builder appeared to her in the form of a bronze statue. Was this a message from the spirit? Was he asking Loli to construct a statue of him on this site as a memorial? Loli believed so. In order to placate the spirit of Waldo Sexton she decided to erect not only a bronze statue of him on the site of his mountain but also a bronze miniature of the mountain itself. Whether or not the City of Vero Beach liked this idea is another question. Things of any height are not appreciated in Florida unless it has to do with peaks on a stock market graph.

SPOOKY TREES

There may be more haunted trees in Florida than anywhere else in the country. Perhaps that is because of the lush vegetation in the Sunshine State and the year-round pleasant climate, which allows for more outdoor activity than in most other states.

The first haunted tree is on the Ferry Pass Highway about a mile outside of old Pensacola. The haunting originates from the late 1700s when the Spanish still had possession of Florida. At that time, the

Spanish were attempting to cut a road through the swamp and pine forests that extended to what is now the northern part of Escambia County. Their work came to an abrupt halt, however, when the last line of trees they felled revealed that they had come upon the Escambia River, which was too wide at that spot for them to ford.

The road-building crew was instructed to set up a more-or-less permanent camp until it was decided how they were to proceed. Among this group of laborers was a Spanish man who had gained possession of several strings of very valuable pearls and a sizable diamond. He placed these valuables in a chest and, with a friend, buried his secret treasure. It was not long before the friend dug up the chest and hid it in a hollow tree. The owner of the valuables discovered the theft and confronted his ex-friend. The two men drew their weapons and in a quick gunfight, the burglar killed the rightful owner of the treasure. It is the spirit of the murdered man that haunts the hollow tree where the treasure had been hidden. He regularly returns to the site with torch in hand in search of the stolen cache of valuables.

Another haunted tree is located not very far from there and dates back to the same era. The ghost belongs to Juan Alverado, a Spanish soldier, who had been transferred from Havana, Cuba to Pensacola in order to help explore the Escambia River, which stood in the path of the road construction.

Alverado and a companion enlisted the aid of a couple of Native Americans to guide them in their explorations. For some reason, the Native American guides turned hostile during the journey and attacked the two Spaniards at a place called 'Cottage Hill Landing.' Alverado's friend was instantly killed and Alverado was severely injured. Despite his wounds, Alverado was able to drag himself to a place of concealment inside a hollow cypress tree where he remained until the Native Americans gave up looking for him and departed. Alvaredo's wounds were so serious that he could not extricate himself from the hollow of the tree and that is where he died.

Since this incident, the ghost of an armored Spanish soldier has been seen at this location. It used to make a yearly appearance at sunset, at which time it would pace about the area of the cypress tree, disappearing only with the last rays of the descending sun. The cypress tree was eventually cut down in 1929 and inside it was found a skeleton in a suit of armor. A proper burial was made of the remains in Pensacola Cemetery and since that time, the apparition has come no more.

Still in the same region—on the shore of Escambia Bay—there is the site of a haunted tree stump. The spirit here also belongs to a Spanish soldier from the 1700s named Juan. He fell in love with the daughter of a local Native American chief and built her a fine marriage lodge of pine saplings. The Native American chief did not approve of their relationship and confronted them near the site of the lodge. While Juan stood embracing the Native American woman, her father unloosed one of his arrows and pierced them both with one shot. Juan and the girl fell dead across the stumps of the pine trees. Their spirits remain here at the spot of their murder, entwined in love among the pines.

Heading south, our search for ghosts takes us once against to the vicinity of Kissimmee and a location near Canoe Creek. Here we come across famous 'Deadman's Oak.' This time the victim was a local resident who was captured by the Spaniards when he was riding the trail between Lake Kissimmee and Lake Gentry. They led him across Canoe Creek bridge to a nearby oak tree. The local was then placed against the tree and had his head cut off. It is to this location that the spirit of the murdered man makes his nightly return in search of his lost head.

CONCLUSION

You have now met many of our Florida ghosts. Most of them are an entertaining and down-to-earth lot. Who could forget the woman who refused to wear undergarments when company came calling or the eccentric architect who built his own tomb and had himself locked inside just days before his death?

One striking peculiarity about the ghosts of Florida is how many of them are located in such close proximity to each other. Take, for example, the numerous ghosts who haunt the Pensacola Naval Yard and Air Station. Note the many spirits who populate the region near the Escambia River, where the Spanish were building a road and take particular notice of how many are hovering around certain trees. Even more striking is the Seville Square area of Pensacola where nearly everyone lives in a haunted house. Why are there so many ghosts to be found in such close proximity to each other? Could this indicate that there are regions in space and time that are more conducive to ghostly activity than others and that spirits find it easier to return to these sites?

We have visited a great many ghosts in these pages and among theme is one of the most well-authenticated spirits that I have ever come across: 'Fink' Finley of the Tampa Theatre. During his life, the theatre was practically his home so why should it be any different after his death? The sightings of the former projectionist are such a common occurrence that his ghost is accepted as almost another member of the current staff.

Another especially interesting account comes from the Catalina Gardens Restaurant where the spirit of the former owner, Catalina, has been seen on a great many occasions. She is always wearing the same white dress and she has been seen in various locations throughout the building.

As we continue to study ghostly phenomena, we continue to get closer to the understanding of its true nature. Perhaps someday we will unlock many of the deper mysteries of hauntings and ghostly behavior. Maybe someday, we will be able to communicate with ghosts through specially designed audio amplifiers. Maybe other means of electro-magnetic communication will be established. If ghosts truly are pure energy it seems likely that someday a device for tuning into this energy will be invented. Maybe someday will be soon.

THE END